The Lightkeeper

About the Authors

A third-generation lighthouse keeper on both sides, *Gerald Butler* joined the Commissioners of Irish Lights in 1969. He spent most of his career as an assistant keeper on Bull Rock, Fastnet Rock, the Old Head of Kinsale and Mizen Head lighthouses.

During his twenty-one years of service, he also served on Dún Laoghaoire East Pier, Roche's Point, Power Head, Wicklow Head, Tuskar Rock, Hook Point, Ballycotton Island, Skellig Michael, Inishtearaght, Eeragh, Eagle Island, Blackrock Mayo, Arranmore, Fanad Head, Rockabill, Roancarrig and the Baily lighthouses.

Born in Castletownbere, today he lives in Rathbarry, near Clonakilty in west Cork. He is the attendant keeper at Galley Head Lighthouse, is a member of the Association of Lighthouse Keepers, and lectures schools and societies on the history of lighthouses.

Patricia Ahern is the author of *Picture Poetry Mallow* and the co-author of *In Search of the Missing*. She has an MA in Women's Studies, a H Dip in Journalism and Media Communications, and a BA in English and Sociology. Born in Mallow, she now lives in Ballinhassig, County Cork and is currently co-writing a biography, *The Loneliest Boy in the World*, with Gearóid Cheaist Ó Catháin, who was the last native child of the Great Blasket and is the only survivor of those evacuated from the island in 1953.

THE LIGHTKEEPER

A Memoir

Gerald Butler *and* Patricia Ahern

The Liffey Press

Published by
The Liffey Press Ltd
Raheny Shopping Centre, Second Floor
Raheny, Dublin 5, Ireland
www.theliffeypress.com

A catalogue record of this book is
available from the British Library.

ISBN 978-1-908308-25-2
Second printing

Printed in Ireland by Sprint Print.

Contents

Foreword

Although the Commissioners of Irish Lights first started to provide and maintain the lighthouses, beacons and navigation buoys just over 200 years ago, Hook Point lighthouse has been warning the few hardy mariners who were about at the time of the dangers of that rocky headland since the fifth century. The Normans landed at Bannoa Bay in County Wexford on 1 May 1169 and built the magnificent Hook Point tower, but their ambitions did not stop at lighting the coastline. The Irish Lights' motto, *In salutem omnium*, meaning 'in the service of all', would have been a wholly inappropriate motto for such ruthless but effective conquerors.

Gerry Butler started to train as a lightkeeper in 1950, which was the year that he and his twin brother Edmund were born. Gerry's father was a lightkeeper and his mother came from a lightkeeper's family. After 61 years, Gerry is still a lightkeeper working at Galley Head lighthouse, where his mother Pauline had spent 34 years. She is still very much alive today. She has 42 grandchildren and 19 great-grandchildren. Since her retirement, she has studied geology. She has travelled to Iceland to carry out fieldwork there. It may be a strange analogy, but you can see from this that if the Butlers were a bottle of wine they would most assuredly be Lafite Rothschild.

The pages which follow this foreword are extraordinary. They will tell of two wild twins growing up in the shadow of a light-

house. It was a hard but independent childhood which was nour-
ished by a loving family. There is much to be learned about the history of lighthouses from the research which Gerry has carried out,
but the unique feature of this book is the stories of the lighthouses
which Gerry kept during his years as a lightkeeper. It was mostly
long watches, hours spent cleaning lenses and the maintenance of
the generators, but the social interactions and the loyalty which
developed between the three keepers on duty also played a part
by maintaining high morale to ensure that mariners would see the
light and hear the fog signal when they came within range. What
Gerry describes no longer exists today, and it is unlikely that it
will ever be replaced. His work is a wonderful insight into a lightkeeper's life, which, throughout its pages, records the deep respect
which the lightkeeper has for his real master, well described by
James Joyce as 'the snot green, the scrotum tightening sea'.

Gerry graphically describes how the Atlantic seas roll on to
the Fastnet Rock from the west, travelling at 50 miles an hour or
more. In storm conditions, as the waves strike the rock, they rise
up and pass right over the dome at the very top of the tower. Gerry
records that in prolonged storm conditions, the Fastnet tower can
shake and sway for a period of up to ten hours. This fascinating
history of a lightkeeper and of his family and fellow keepers re-
calls the past and, as such, Gerry's book is a wonderful record of a
unique piece of social history. If, in years to come, some distracted
lunatic writes the history of the life of a virtual buoy, it will not
compare. The lights will go out and the mariner will be ushered
away from danger by virtual navigation lanes plotted on an electronic chart. Our bow is headed on that course.

John Gore-Grimes
Commissioner of Irish Lights

To all the lightkeepers, especially to my own
family line. I am eternally grateful that I was born
to serve in the Irish Lights as a lightkeeper.
– *Gerald Butler*

"When you get into a tight place and everything
goes against you, till it seems as though you
could not hang on a minute longer, never give up
then, for that is just the place and time that the
tide will turn." – *Harriet Beecher Stowe*

Commissioners of Irish Lights
Principal Aids to Navigation provided

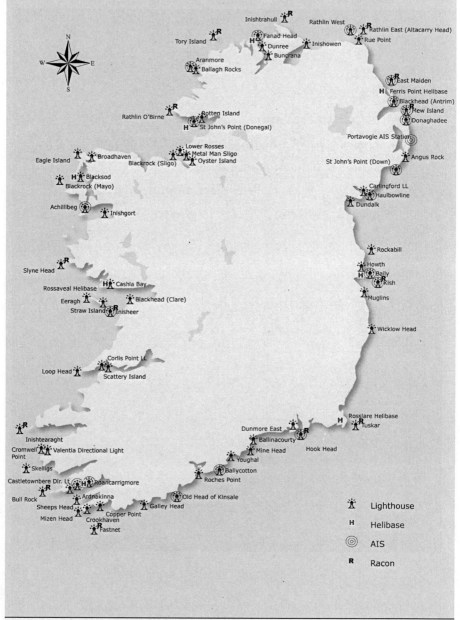

Inishtrahull

Tory Island

Rathlin West

Rathlin East (Altacarry Head)

Fanad Head

Rue Point

Dunree

Buncrana

Inishowen

Aranmore

Ballagh Rocks

East Maiden

Ferris Point Helibase

Blackhead (Antrim)

Mew Island

Donaghadee

Rathlin O'Birne

Rotten Island

St John's Point (Donegal)

Portavogie AIS Station

Lower Rosses

Metal Man Sligo

Oyster Island

Eagle Island

Broadhaven

Blackrock (Sligo)

St John's Point (Down)

Angus Rock

Blacksod

Blackrock (Mayo)

Carlingford LL

Haulbowline

Dundalk

Achillbeg

Inishgort

Rockabill

Howth

Bailly

Kish

Muglins

Slyne Head

Rossaveal Helibase

Cashla Bay

Eeragh

Blackhead (Clare)

Straw Island Inisheer

Wicklow Head

Corlis Point LL

Loop Head

Scattery Island

Rosslare Helibase

Tuskar

Dunmore East

Inishtearaght

Ballinacourty

Mine Head

Hook Head

Cromwell

Valentia Directional Light

Point

Youghal

Skelligs

Ballycotton

Roches Point

Castletownbere Dir. Lt.

Roancarrigmore

Old Head of Kinsale

Bull Rock

Ardnakinna

Galley Head

Sheeps Head

Copper Point

Mizen Head

Crookhaven

Fastnet

Lighthouse

H Helibase

AIS

R Racon

Prologue

On Monday, the fog cleared at 8.45 a.m. and the wind registered at southerly force 3. A woman named Mrs Good rang Fastnet Rock and asked me if she could come out to the rock by boat to watch the yachts circling the lighthouse. I warned her against it, as the wind had begun to freshen and the fog had cleared very quickly. Both conditions together indicated that the weather was about to change for the worst. Around 2.00 p.m., the wind shifted to south-south-east and increased to strength 4.

On Fastnet, we kept a close eye out for the yachts. About 4.00 p.m., as the wind shifted again to southerly force 4, the first of the vessels sailed into view and began to round the lighthouse. These yachts were huge and rated among the biggest of the fleet. They would have gained great ground as the freshening, south-easterly winds would have blown them forward and increased their pace.

As evening approached, the winds grew stronger. Our radio on Fastnet broke down. Luckily, an Irish Lights helicopter happened to be in Castletownbere and delivered a new radio to the rock, which was a radio telephone transmitter and receiver, in medium frequency, with a range of about 150 miles. While we awaited the new radio, we kept contact with the keepers on Mizen Head by telephone. Once the new radio arrived, we resumed radio contact with them straight away.

At 6.00 p.m., the wind shifted back to south-south-east and increased to force 6. A small, wooden, pleasure craft sailed out to

Fastnet from Crookhaven to observe the yachts rounding Fastnet. The weather deteriorated rapidly and the wind strengthened. The sea raged and the rise and fall of the waves varied between 10 and 15 feet. Standing on the balcony of the Fastnet, I watched the small vessel for hours through my binoculars, as it tried to take shelter on the rough sea. It was the only boat in sight. Since the passing of the first, large, race yachts, no other yacht had reached the Fastnet, which suggested that the remainder lagged far behind the leaders.

I continued to watch the small boat as it struggled on the sea. At first, it sailed under the Fastnet. Then, it drifted eastwards and headed towards Cape Clear Island, about three miles east of the Fastnet. But I was unsure if the craft was actually in difficulty, as it seemed to be keeping its head up against the weather. At 8.00 p.m., the wind increased to gale force 8 and it began to rain. Conditions deteriorated further.

At 10.00 p.m., the lights of the small vessel disappeared and the boat went out of sight. I became alarmed and immediately contacted Baltimore Lifeboat by telephone. The secretary's wife, Eileen Bushe, answered the call. She listened attentively to my concern. When I requested to have the lifeboat launched to search for the vessel, she said that it was already on the ocean, as a boat with an RTÉ press crew on board had failed to return to Schull at the expected time. On that fateful night, the members of the lifeboat crew who took to the seas were: Christy Collins, coxswain; Pat Harrington, acting second coxswain; Michael O'Connell, mechanic; John O'Regan, assistant mechanic; Noel Cottrell, second assistant mechanic; Paul O'Regan; Dan Cahalane; and Kieran Cotter. Although the lifeboat *The Robert* scoured the ocean in search of the small vessel, it failed to find the missing boat.

As the lifeboat began making its way back to Crookhaven, some of the racing yachts sailed into view near Fastnet. By now, the storm was raging and the sea thrashed 55 feet high against the entrance door of the lighthouse. We locked up and battened down all our storm doors. We had no fear for our own safety, as we had experienced much harsher conditions in winter time. But we were now becoming increasingly concerned for the three thousand competitors in the race, many of whom had small vessels, no radios and may have been inexperienced in sailing on enormous seas in stormy weather.

In the lighthouse, we had an Aldis lamp, which we used for Morse code by light at night and which could throw a bright beam over a distance of several miles. Now, we used it to read the sail numbers on the yachts as they rounded Fastnet. We sent the information to Mizen Head lightkeepers by radio and they forwarded it to Cowes by telephone.

Sometimes, when we shone the Aldis lamp on the yachts, a massive wave battered against the rock and blotted out our view, allowing us to see only a huge volume of water, sweeping forcefully right over the rock, leaving merely the top of the tower visible. We took no notice of the onslaught and continued to shine our light on the yachts.

At 11.00 p.m., conditions worsened. The sea rose higher and higher and battered against the rock at a height of 80 feet. The wind reached strong gale force 9. As the yachts continued to round the Fastnet, the crews battled hard to control their boats. The number of people on each yacht varied, depending on the size of the boat. On average, crews probably numbered between six and nine.

At midnight, the wind shifted again from south-south-east to southerly and increased to storm force 10. At fifteen minutes past midnight, we started sounding the fog horn. To the mariners struggling for their lives on the tempestuous sea, its high-pitched blare must have sounded like a siren from hell.

1

One Life

My father was a lighthouse keeper and that shaped my childhood. Being one of fifteen children and having an identical twin also played a part. My twin brother and I always stuck together, dressed the same and shared everything. Sometimes, I felt we had only one life, not two, as my life was his and his life was mine.

When Edmund and I were born in the summer of 1950, Daddy was working as an assistant keeper on Roancarrig lighthouse near Castletownbere in west Cork, with the Commissioners of Irish Lights – which is the lighthouse authority for all of Ireland and commonly known as Irish Lights. Roancarrig was a rock station, which meant it was surrounded by water and detached from the mainland. Daddy spent three weeks at the lighthouse and one at home, while we lived on the mainland, on the outskirts of Castletownbere, with Mammy and our older brother Lawrence, in a block of spacious, two-storey houses. These houses stood out from all the other houses in the town, as a flag flew on a mast in front of them, showing a lighthouse and a lightship in opposite diagonal quadrants, with the red Saint George's cross in the centre, marking them out as the homes of lighthouse families. Inside, the walls were painted in brown at the base and yellow above, with a thin, red, dado line splitting both shades.

Even though Mammy had grown up as the daughter of a lighthouse keeper, she found it hard coping with Daddy's absence, which she often described as a prison sentence. But her loneliness

4

ended when Daddy was transferred to Galley Head lighthouse, near Clonakilty – a station built in 1875, during the heyday of lighthouse building in Ireland, and connected to the mainland by a peninsula. Galley Head had two adjoining, rectangular houses, linked to the lighthouse by a long corridor. As an added bonus for Mammy, her father was already installed there as the principal keeper. My father and my grandfather had previously worked together at Eagle Island lighthouse, off the Mayo coast, and it was there that my parents fell in love.

When we moved to Galley Head, Edmund and I were only two years of age and still very much under the watchful eye of our mother. We were now living on a cliff top, about 133 feet above Saint George's Channel, overlooking Rosscarbery Bay and enclosed by a boundary cliff wall. But living next door to our grandparents gave us some extra scope. Every chance we got, we ran in and out to them and rummaged in their cupboards for sweets and biscuits.

It was the age of the rural electrification scheme and one day ESB workers came to the headland, dug a hole six feet deep for an electricity pole and disappeared. Later, while Mammy stood chatting to one of the lighthouse keepers, Edmund ran over to the hole and jumped in. I followed and plunged down after him. When Mammy heard the screams of terror coming from the hole, she summoned my grandfather, who quickly came to our rescue and pulled us out.

While sounds of the sea, ships and nature echoed all around us, my abiding memory is the shrill of the whistle pipe, which was connected from the lighthouse to our parents' upstairs bedroom and was blown as a cry for help or a signal that it was time to change watch.

Like the flashing beam at the top of the lighthouse, nothing was ever static for the lighthouse keepers and their families. After only two years at Galley Head, Daddy was moved to a rock station on Ballycotton Island in east Cork, which had shore dwellings for the keepers' families in the fishing village of Ballycotton. He resumed the old routine of three weeks on the rock and one week ashore. Now, we were living near Mammy's uncles, aunts and cousins, as her father was a native of Ballycotton. But she still missed Daddy in his absence.

When Edmund and I started at the local, four-teacher school, we were wild with energy and excitement. Every morning before school, we waited outside our gate at Power's Terrace for our friend Dominic O'Connor, the son of another assistant keeper. Dominic had a toy aeroplane, three inches long, and the three of us would charge down the street, pretending to be taking off in the plane. By the time we reached school, we were buzzing.

One morning, when our teacher, Mrs Geary, failed to calm us, she threatened to take Edmund in to her husband's classroom. Once I saw her catching Edmund by the arm to take him away, I leaped up out of my seat, snatched his other arm, began a tug of war with her and screamed, 'No! He's not going in!'

On our way home from school, we never passed Tadhg O'Driscoll's slaughter house without lying flat on the ground and peeping under the door to see if he was killing a cow. As children, we thought of it as entertainment and never had an ounce of pity for the animals.

One of our favourite people was Guard Conium. Edmund and I would stand up on the gate and watch for him, as our street was part of his regular beat. He never passed us by without stopping to give us a blow of his whistle.

Our elderly, next-door neighbour Bob Mahony spoiled us. He ran the post office with his wife and daughter Ethel and was the honorary secretary of Ballycotton Lifeboat. Bob would take us for a drive in his Ford Anglia, often to Cloyne, or wherever he happened to be going to do some shopping. Edmund and I would stand up on the trunk of the drive shaft, beaming from ear to ear, waving to anyone we passed, proud as punch to be whizzing by and dizzy out of our minds with excitement, knowing that Bob would treat us to a bag of multi-coloured, hard-boiled sweets, or maybe some sticky toffees.

Whenever we got wind of the fact that the commissioners from Irish Lights were due to pay their annual tour of inspection, we knew we were in for more treats, as they always brought us sweets. Our house became a hive of activity, with Mammy dusting, scrubbing and polishing all around her. On the day of the visit, Edmund and I would stand like statues, dressed in our Sunday clothes, on our best behaviour, trying not to talk until the commissioners spoke to us first. They usually patted us on the head and said something like, 'My, you've grown a lot since last year.' Or, they might ask, 'How are you getting on at school?' Dinner was always put on hold until they left, as Mammy wanted everything gleaming, even the pots and pans.

Mammy was in her glory as our First Holy Communion drew near. Like her mother, who was a seamstress, she was good with a needle and thread. We saw her cut out paper patterns for our new, beige suits, pin them to the flattened-out material and then carefully trim off the edges. She delighted in the fact that she was able to make the suits herself and when her relatives popped in for a chat, she threw back her head, laughed aloud and told in her native, Antrim accent how she was up half the night sewing the pieces together, which she did on her shiny, black, Singer sewing machine. Edmund and I hated all the fuss and dreaded having to stand on the kitchen table, day after day, as she cheerfully fitted, measured and altered the outfits, stuck pins all over us and admired us from every angle. Often, Mammy's aunts were called in to give their opinion. They eyed us up and down, prodded us, twirled us around in every direction and spoke about us to Mammy as if we weren't there. Then, when the big day came, Edmund and I thought it would never end, as we were fed up of posing for photographs and trying to hold a smile without squinting our eyes.

No matter what happened, the highlight for us was always Daddy's return from the rock. We'd count down the days to his homecoming and hop up on a kitchen chair to tick off each day on the religious calendar hanging on the wall. On the night before his arrival, we'd lie restless in bed, twisting and turning, unable to sleep, bursting with excitement. Then, on the day of his return, we'd stand on the gate for hours, stretching our necks, wanting to be the first to spot him coming over the hill from the pier. And then he'd come into view, dressed in his smart, double-breasted, navy-blue uniform, with two rows of gleaming, brass buttons and topped off with a matching, peaked cap. We'd race up the hill, dance around him and breathlessly gush out every bit of our news, all in one go. Having him back was like winning a prize in a raffle – the best prize – and we'd hurry him down the hill, eager to bring him home as fast as we could to Mammy. Once Mammy had put his dinner on the table, he'd give us a penny each. We'd dash off to the shop and tell everyone we met that our father was home.

One particular homecoming in Ballycotton stands out in my mind. Daddy had only just arrived home and Edmund and I perched ourselves on the kitchen table, keen to savour the moment. Daddy put his arms around Mammy and kissed her. Then, they hugged tightly and held onto each other for what seemed like an eternity. A feeling of warmth swept over me.

While Daddy was away, Mammy took on the roles of mother and father to us. But once he returned, she stepped back a little and gave him back his place in the family. Although he could be very serious when it came to making decisions, most of the time he was jovial and witty.

During his week at home, Daddy played with us a lot. He knew how to entertain us and keep us busy. One day, he bought a big bag of nails and taught us how to hammer a nail into a huge plank in the back yard. It amused us for hours and made us feel like big, strong men. But he had many chores to do too, especially as we had now grown to a family of eight children.

Edmund and I watched him as he worked and he taught us everything he knew. He trimmed our hair with a manual clippers, a task most lighthouse keepers did for each other while out on the rock. Dressed in his dark, leather apron, he mended our shoes, a skill he learned from our next-door neighbour John Crowley, a former shoemaker, when both of them served at the lighthouse together. Edmund and I stood at either side of Daddy as he soled our shoes with material from a 'bend' of leather, which came from the hide of a cow. The beige strip measured about three feet by five feet and was a quarter of an inch thick. First, he softened a lump of wax by rubbing it in his hands. Then, he spun layers of hemp on a hand twist-drill, drew out the wax, pulled the hemp through it to make it into a thick, waterproof thread and rolled the hemp up and down his leg, until he twisted it into a 12-foot length. He cut a channel and bored a hole into the sole of the shoe with an awl, attached the hemp to both ends of a soft, pliable pig's bristle bone and then used the bone as a needle to draw the hemp tightly through the shoe and new sole, while the oozing wax sealed up the hole. Then, he tapped all around the sole with a hammer, trimmed the edges with a knife and rubbed the shoe with a heel-ball, to darken the new edge and seal the gap.

Daddy even knew how to make a pair of shoes. He had three different anvils, known as lasts. These flat, heavy, steel moulds bore the inside shape of a shoe and Daddy had one for a large shoe, a small shoe and a heel.

Every Saturday night, he polished and shined our shoes and lined them up in the hallway, sparkling and ready for Mass the following morning. Then, he stood back, folded his arms and said, 'Isn't that a grand sight now,' as he always took great pride in everything he did.

We knew Daddy helped people at sea to find their position in relation to the lighthouse, by flashing the beacon and blasting the fog horn. Other than that we knew very little about his work. He never spoke to us about his life on the rock and any information we gathered about it was only by chance, when we happened to overhear the adults talking. One night, we heard him tell Mammy's uncle that drinking water was a big problem at the lighthouse, due to long spells of dry weather, and that when it dried up a big ship called *Granuaile* sailed to the lighthouse with supplies.

One morning, Daddy announced out of the blue that he was taking Edmund out to the rock with him for one week and me the following week. My heart sank, as I wanted him to take the two of us together. Up until then, we had never spent time apart. I begged Daddy to take me too, but Mammy insisted that I stay at home, as she said Daddy would be unable to mind us both.

I watched Edmund walk up the hill with Daddy, hand-in-hand. As they disappeared over the top, I felt that part of me was being ripped away. That night, before I went to bed, I stood in front of the mirror and stared at myself. I pretended I was looking at Edmund. Somehow, it comforted me. But for the rest of the week, I felt lonely. I was lost without him and had no mind for food or play. At the same time, I was looking forward to my own trip.

When my turn came to go to the rock, I was brimming over with delight. Mammy had often taken us older children on a Sunday, day trip to the lighthouse, on the small, open, timber, motor boat that went over and back with visitors, but I had never before stayed there. I couldn't wait.

As the boat backed away from Ballycotton, I looked up in wonder at the vastness of the pier, which never failed to amaze me, then down at the endless depth of the water. As we sped further away from the pier and the water swirled all around the boat, the land we left behind paled into insignificance.

When we set foot on Ballycotton Island, which rises 150 feet above sea level, I gazed up at the lighthouse, sitting firmly on top of a steep slope, alone, showing off its black lantern and enclosed by gleaming, white walls. I knew it well, because of the day trips with Mammy, but now I wondered if the waves might sneak over the top of the lighthouse while I was asleep or if pirates might land and kidnap me. Deep down I knew that would never happen, because Daddy or one of the other keepers would keep a close watch on the sea.

All through the week, Daddy protected me from the dangers of living on a cliff. He was willing to let me explore, but only within the walls surrounding the lighthouse. Exploring without Edmund was no fun. So, I followed Daddy everywhere instead. Together, we weeded the garden, tended to the vegetable patch, gathered eggs from the hens and milked the goats. One of the goats was a cross billy-goat. He kept banging against us and Daddy told me that the only way to get rid of him was to give him a lighted cigarette. Once Daddy lit up a cigarette and popped it into the goat's mouth, he left us alone.

I watched Daddy check that the water was safe to drink. He filled a mug of water from the catch pit at the top of the water tank and spilled a drop on top of the hot range. If the water left a white mark after drying, he knew there was salt in it, caused by the spray of huge waves. Straight away, he allowed the salted water on the catch pit to flow away. Once the fresh water showed up as being clear, he opened the tanks and left in the water for storage. A small cardboard hung permanently over the fireplace, stating if the tanks were open or closed, so that any keeper starting a shift would know the state of play.

Daddy showed me how to do semaphore, which is a way of sending messages in daytime by using hand flags. Usually, the flags are yellow and red, with both colours split diagonally. Each position at which the flag is held in the air stands for a certain letter or number. Daddy told me that messages sent by semaphore could be picked up through a telescope at a distance of 16 miles away.

At night, he taught me Morse code by using a torch. Morse code is a means of sending written information through a series of on-off tones, lights or clicks. A sequence of dots and dashes represent each letter of the alphabet and numbers. A fast flash symbolises a dot, while a long flash signifies a dash. All dashes must be the same size and the spaces between each flash must be uniform in time. I held Daddy's torch and practised pressing the button to make the letter 'A', which is represented by a dot and a dash. Once I mastered that, I moved on to another letter.

Daddy told me that when a ship came into view of the lighthouse at night, it timed and recorded the number of the lighthouse's flashes, together with the number of flashes per minute. By checking the sequence with the 'Admiralty Marine Chart', or the 'Admiralty Lists of Lights', the mariners could confirm their location in relation to each lighthouse and identify any hidden dangers. To distinguish one lighthouse from another, each station has its own individual light flashing character. Like the other keepers, Daddy had to do his four-hour night watch to keep the equipment that rotated the light wound up and to attend to the light lamp.

When a fog set in, Daddy started the air compressors. These huge Ruston and Hornsby 3XHR horizontal cylinder engines, with their heavy four-foot by six-inch cast-iron wheel, were directly joined to twin vertical cylinder compressors that delivered 108 cubic feet of air per minute. The air was pumped into eight, big, steel, round, air-receiver storage tanks. With their engines running and the air in the receivers reaching the required pressure, the valves opened and, by means of a timing machine set to the lighthouse's character blasting sequence, the air was delivered to the diaphone, or siren. Then, amplified by the huge cast-iron horn, the diaphone's deafening, droning sound, which ended in a descending grunt, blasted over the ocean.

Every day, Daddy read to me a lot, as he was big into reading and stashed stacks upon stacks of books in the keepers' house to while away his free time. We sat by the black, steel Larbert range, which was set into the chimney, and he filled me with stories about lighthouses and told me that Ballycotton lighthouse was built to prevent more wreckage after the paddle steamship *Sirius* – the first steam vessel to cross the Atlantic Ocean in April 1838 – crashed onto Smith's Rock, south-west of Ballycotton, in 1847, in dense fog. When Captain Moffatt tried to run the ship into Ballycotton Harbour, it became a total wreck.

Sometimes, I felt I was living in a limbo. Inside the lighthouse, I felt safe, as smug as a bug, as if nothing could harm me. But outside seemed threatening, as the waves below constantly crashed and swirled and made loud, rhythmic sounds. Whenever I heard noises coming over the sea from the mainland, I felt like I was in an in-between place, apart, but still connected.

Every night, I was glad to share Daddy's bed as the darkness outside scared me. Apart from the flash of the light beam, everything was pitch-black. The house was infested with ants and I was afraid of them too. But Daddy told me they could not get into my bed, as the iron bed-posts stood in four bean tins of water, to keep them away,

My stay ended a day early, because Mammy got word to the lighthouse that Edmund was lost without me. When I went home, Edmund and I stayed awake all night, whispering excitedly about all we had seen and heard at the lighthouse and laughing our heads off about the smoking billy-goat. We shared the bedroom with Lawrence. He told us to go to sleep, but we were too excited. Even then, Edmund and I knew we would both be lightkeepers. It seemed only natural.

Every day, from then on, Morse code and semaphore became part of our everyday play. We stood on the front wall and pretended we were on the cliff top, looking out to sea. We waved yellow and red flags, which Mammy had sewn together from remnants. Then, at nightfall, we flashed our torches, full of enthusiasm. None of the ships would crash on the rocks. Our messages would save them all.

But, being part of a big family, we had jobs to do too. Along with some of our brothers and sisters, we took it in turn to clear the table after meals, wash or dry the ware, tidy up and sweep the floor.

At meal times, the whole family sat down together. Each of us had our own place at the kitchen table and we fought hard to keep it. We ate what we were given and never complained or asked for anything special. Once a week, we were given a sugar stick as a treat, which was a long, twirled, sweet stick that took ages to suck.

After working more than five years on Ballycotton Island, Daddy was transferred to Dundalk Pile lighthouse, four miles from Dundalk and half-way out in Dundalk Bay, on the east coast. One day, Edmund and I sailed out to the lighthouse with Paddy Macken, the boatman contracted to take relief keepers in and out. Paddy told us that on spring tides the strand dried out to beyond the lighthouse and that music drifting across the sea from the seaside village of Blackrock at night could be heard on the station, which stood on round, steel columns embedded in the sand. When we arrived, Daddy appeared above us and lowered down a rope, which Paddy tied around our waists for safety. Then, Edmund and I climbed up to the lighthouse on a ladder, which was almost vertical.

As the accommodation at the lighthouse was confined, Daddy worked only three days on the rock and spent two days at home, followed by three days at the lighthouse and three days ashore. Our lives changed big time. Moving to a big, busy, industrial town

14

and adapting to an urban environment placed a huge strain on Mammy, as she now found it harder to control the family, especially Edmund and me, and missed the support of her relatives. Edmund and I fell in with the wrong crowd and joined a gang of stone-throwing, brawling youths. We pelted the enemy gangs, wrestled with them and chased them through the streets, yelling at the top of our voices. When Daddy was on the lighthouse, we slipped out at night, stayed out as late as we could and terrorised our neighbours. We ran from house to house, knocking on doors, ringing doorbells, shouting through letterboxes, and then raced out of sight to avoid being caught. When we came home, we lied to Mammy about where we had been.

One day, a garda called to our door and complained about us to Mammy. When Daddy came home, we overheard Mammy tell him she couldn't manage the two of us. Daddy pounded his fist on the table and said firmly, 'Right! We're getting out of here.'

In no time at all, Daddy was moved to Mine Head lighthouse, on a headland in County Waterford. Located on a high cliff top, the 69-foot tower boasts the highest light above sea-level in Ireland. Our new home was one of the two, spacious, storey-and-a-half cottages, designed by George Halpin, the famous engineer, with sky lights, gable windows and low-hanging upstairs ceilings. Our parents' bedroom was fitted with battery-powered alarm bells. These were linked to the lighthouse by telephone wire and sounded a sharp, piercing noise when the lighthouse beam failed. The station also had stores, a workshop, and a timber dwelling house for any young, trainee keeper, who was known as a supernumerary assistant keeper, or SAK, and usually came for a stint of three weeks.

Edmund and I gasped at our new-found freedom. We sensed that we were isolated from the rest of the world and protected from it by the high boundary wall, which made the area around the lighthouse look like a fort. Being small, everything around us seemed huge. We were dazzled by the vast space and emptiness before our eyes, knowing that the prospect of thrills and adventure lay right on our doorstep.

We quickly teamed up with our next-door neighbour Stephen Stocker, the youngest child of the principal keeper and his wife. Stephen had a roguish pair of eyes and a brain for mechanics. All belonging to him were masters at engineering. Our older brother Lawrence had no interest in joining our gang. Instead, he stayed indoors and read, as he was mad for books, just like Daddy.

Stephen, Edmund and I spent all our time outdoors, running wild all over the cliff, playing hurling, football and cowboys and Indians. A triangular outhouse for animals, with a cobbled floor, a high wall in front and a garden, became our fort. We marked it as our territory by erecting a pole and flying a yellow duster on top. We prepared for an attack by the Indians and watched through the narrow slits in the walls for their approach. Sometimes, we held shoot-outs to find out which of us was the fastest with a gun. Two of us would stand back to back, with our toy guns in our holsters and our hands by our sides. Then we'd walk ahead ten paces, turn around, draw out our guns and fire.

One day, Edmund and I stood up on the balcony rail, with a drop of 120 feet below us. We walked around it in opposite directions, passed each other out and ended up back where we started. Of course Stephen always had to go a step further. So he climbed over the railing, hung on to the rails with his hands and swung as fast as he could from one to the other.

When Stephen's father was transferred back to his Galway roots, Pa Crowley, a loud, tall, strong Youghal man and a veteran of the First World War, took his place. Our lives changed completely, as we were older, wilder and even more eager for adventure. Edmund and I couldn't believe our luck when Pa showed us his Point 22 rifle and his pump action shotgun, which could be pumped to eject a used round of ammunition and to load a new one. We now had a hero in our midst, a real hero, and we latched onto him, not wanting to let him out of our sight. Every day after dinner, we climbed the cliffs and walked the fields with Pa, often not returning until dusk. We shot at everything in sight, birds, seals, even basking sharks, as they often came to the surface for plankton. Then at night, Pa would sit by the roaring fire in the kitchen, chatting to Mammy, while the rest of us played games or argued with each other. Any time Edmund and I pestered Pa to tell us what it was like to stick a bayonet in somebody during the World War, he fell silent.

One morning after a fierce storm, Edmund and I scoured the cliffs to check for damage. We spotted a massive hole, as a huge, overhanging boulder, the size of a small building, had become dislodged, tumbled down and dug out a gigantic crevasse, about 100 feet long, in the face of the cliff. Edmund and I used to spend ages looking down at the hole and throwing stones into it. The stones always landed right at the bottom of the crevasse, as there was no grass on it. We decided it would make a great slide and knew exactly the best time to try it out.

Daddy was always a man of routine and went to bed for a rest at the same time every day, to make up for sleep lost while on the night shift. When Daddy was having one of his naps, Edmund and I prepared for our descent into the hole. I stood into the crevasse first, at chest height, and tried to hold onto the loose ground around me. I was ready for take-off when I suddenly realised that once I began to slide, I'd swiftly gain speed, be unable to stop myself, crash onto the rocks and drown. It was a near-death experience and I quickly climbed out of the hole, with the loose ground swiftly falling away all around me. I was shaken to the core. To this day, I often wonder how I managed to get out of that crumbling cliff.

One day, Edmund and I spotted a dark grey, fat seal, about four feet long, down at the landing base. We rushed breathlessly into

Pa's kitchen and pleaded with him to give us his rifle and one bullet. We dared not ask for more than one, as we knew Pa was thrifty with the bullets. Pa looked down at us and said loudly, 'Yes now, what do you call it?' which was a meaningless saying of his, and he reluctantly handed us the gun and bullet. By the time we climbed down to the landing, the seal had gone underwater.

We decided to return the bullet to Pa, knowing that it might stand us in good stead if we needed one some other time. Then on the way back to Pa's, we spotted our younger brother Jimmy walking in the football field, with his back to an ESB pole. I put the stock of the loaded gun into my tummy, cocked it and squeezed the trigger. By letting the firing pin in slowly, the bullet would not discharge and I could eject it from the gun. Unexpectedly, the pin slipped out of my fingers and the bullet buried itself in the ESB pole, with Jimmy only five paces away. Edmund and I never handled a gun again for a long time.

Shortly after Pa's arrival, we got our first television. Before that we'd been big radio listeners and always tuned in with Daddy to massive events, like when Alan Shepherd became the first American in space or when Sonny Liston took on Cassius Clay. We knew Henry Cooper had a problem with his eyes and on the night he put Clay on the canvas, we went wild. Pa got a great kick out of the television and could mimic the advertisements to perfection. Any time Edmund and I put the kettle on the range to make him a cup of tea, he'd stand in front of us, straighten up his shoulders, take a deep breath and imitate a tea commercial, 'Tea? I like a proper cup of tea.' Edmund and I would fall about the place laughing.

As well as buying a television, Daddy also bought a new, turquoise-blue Station Wagon, which he purchased from Abernethy's in Castlemartyr. It was both a luxury and a necessity, as we lived four miles from the school. Edmund and I smelled its newness and crawled on our hands and knees to check underneath. We drove everywhere with Daddy, eager to learn all we could about the ignition, gears, lights and engine. We always sat in the back seat, perched at either side by the window. Then, when Mammy started to drive, Daddy sent us along to help her. We kept a close eye on her, told her when to change gears, taught her how to dim the lights and warned her to pull up the handbrake when she stopped on a hill. The Station Wagon became our pride and joy. We painted the underneath in white lead to protect it from the salt water. Every Saturday morning, we washed the car religiously with a stirrup pump. We placed the brass pump into a bucket of water. Then I stood on the lower part of the pump and pumped the water out through a hose to Edmund. Every day when school finished, we ran out excitedly, knowing that Daddy would be waiting to drive us home.

The school was located in the Gaeltacht area of Ring and Edmund and I had become fluent Irish speakers, as speaking English at school was forbidden, apart from during the English language class. As an incentive to speak Irish, £5 was awarded annually to every child living in a Gaeltacht area who spoke Irish at school and at home. With a family of twelve children at the time, this extra money was a welcome bonus for Mammy and Daddy. Our school principal, Cyril Farrell, ran an anti-smoking campaign, based on the book *John Joe Fag*, which was full of colourful sketches and listed all the reasons not to smoke. It turned us against smoking for life. Most days at school, the lads raved about television westerns, like *Wagon Train* and *The Virginian*. They never shut up about Trampas, Judge Garth and the rest of the gun-slinging Shiloh men. Edmund and I couldn't see the attraction. In our minds, there was nothing more thrilling and adventurous than hanging around the lighthouse.

In contrast to feeling carefree while roaming the cliffs or spinning around in the Station Wagon, we felt constrained at school. We rebelled against the system by skipping homework, fighting with the other lads and giving cheeky answers to the teachers, who found us unmanageable and were now down on us like a ton of bricks

One day, when we hopped into the Station Wagon after school, Daddy announced he was being transferred, as Mine Head had been electrified and was no longer a two-keeper station. Our eyes and ears popped. Knowing that the teachers were on the verge of complaining us to our parents or expelling us, we needed a bailout – and now we had it.

Once all the packing was done, Mammy and Daddy set off in the Station Wagon with our brothers and sisters. Edmund and I climbed into the removal lorry with the driver, impatient to leave and bursting with excitement. Our time at Mine Head had been full of fun and adventure. Yet, as the lorry pulled slowly away from the cliff top, we never looked back.

2

Into the West

Going back to Galley Head in west Cork must have been like a homecoming for Mammy and Daddy. As Edmund and I were only four years of age when we left there, we had little recollection of the cliff top. We gazed at the lighthouse and two adjoining houses full of wonder and expectation, as if we were seeing them for the very first time. The boundary walls were much lower than at Mine Head and now we had a sense of belonging to the outside world, rather than of being isolated from it, as we could see the water and land around us. Having arrived in late afternoon, we quickly emptied the lorry and piled all our belongings on the front garden, apart from some essentials for the night. All the lighthouse dwellings came fully furnished, but we had our own mattresses and countless wooden boxes, full to the brim with everything we owned. At Mine Head, the lighthouse beacon flashed only out to sea, but at Galley Head, when darkness fell, the lighthouse beam twinkled into our home, bathing it in a warm, welcoming glow.

Daddy enrolled Lawrence at the secondary school in Clonakilty, which was 10 miles from our home. As Edmund and I were showing signs of being good with our hands, he signed us up at the technical school in the town.

On our first day, when the Irish teacher walked into the classroom, Edmund and I were play-acting, holding down one of the lads under his desk. The teacher stood in front of us and threw questions at us in Irish about where we lived and where we had gone to school. He was blown away by our replies and gob-smacked that we were fluent Irish speakers. His face lit up and he chatted with us, full of enthusiasm, while the rest of the lads looked on in bafflement, with no idea of what we were saying. Yet, we fitted right in with them all, as we always made friends easily and they never judged us.

But changing from an Irish-speaking school to an English-speaking school was hard, as we still thought in Irish. When we did maths, we translated everything to Irish in our heads. We found geography especially tough, as the names of places were totally different to what we had learned before. We were fascinated to be taught about agricultural science, chemistry and biology, and excited to be working with metal, timber and electricity, all practical lessons that would later stand well to us as lightkeepers and make us self-sufficient.

As time went by, we returned to our old, mischievous ways. We skipped homework and confused teachers about our identity. Being identical, even our parents failed to tell us apart sometimes, especially when we were sleeping, although Mammy once said that one of our foreheads was slightly more rounded than the other.

After sitting an exam at school, one of the teachers decided we should be separated and placed in different classes. Even though we had sat at opposite ends of the classroom for the test, the teacher believed we had copied, as we had both chosen the same questions to answer and made the same mistakes.

Every morning, we arrived at school with a pellet gun we had got from a cousin in Wexford, unknown to our parents. I stuck the wooden stock under my jumper and fitted it down through the waist of my trousers, while Edmund hid the barrel, which he bent in two, down his trousers and up under his arm. We made the pellets ourselves, out of left-over, ESB, aluminium wire from the lighthouse. Then at lunch hour, the two of us headed off with our friend Louis O'Leary to the nearby fields. Louis had his own pellet gun and we fired at everything in view, including crows, sparrows, linnets and rabbits. But we never managed to shoot down anything, as the guns were weak and the pellets were too light. At night, we hid the gun in the sitting-room, behind some skirting board, onto which we'd placed a hinge and a secret locking device. Years later, when tradesmen came to renovate the Galley, they discovered the hiding place and became very excited, much to our amusement, as they expected to find some hidden treasure.

Often, we brought jam jars to school full of an explosive mixture, made up of sodium chlorate and sugar. Galley Head always stocked a large supply of chlorate, which the station used as a weed killer. At lunch hour, we threw a lighted match into the glass jars, flung them high and watched, electrified, as they exploded like thunder in the air. We also fired bombs over the cliffs. One day, one of the bombs exploded on a grassy part of the cliff and set it alight. We raced to one of the outhouses as fast as we could, grabbed two shovels and climbed down the cliff to batter out the fire before we were caught.

At home, Edmund and I made dagger knives and later brandished them at school. Then we competed against each other to see who could throw a knife the furthest and lodge it into the ground or onto a post.

In the afternoon, we often skipped school and headed for the town dump. We pulled parts from abandoned cars and stored them in a chest of drawers in our bedroom, having piled all our clothes on the floor. We filled the place with junk from the dump. We restored life to an old, broken indicator by connecting it to a battery and we watched with pride as its arm lit up and popped up. We mended an old alarm clock that had lost its ring. Every morning, we always tried to get up early to go shooting on the cliffs, so before we fixed the clock, each of us used to take it in turns at bed time to tie a twine onto one of our big toes, run it down the side

23

of the bed, under all the rubbish on the floor, out the window, and onto the end of a down-pipe. Then, before 6.00 a.m. each morning, one of the supernumeraries on relief at the Galley would tug the twine to wake us. As we'd be in the middle of a deep sleep, we'd wake up suddenly, wondering what was happening, as by now the supernumerary would have pulled the twined foot half way up the window. Then, we'd signal to him that we were up – even though we knew he'd be breaking his sides laughing at the other end – and he'd head off to his bed before schedule, knowing we'd extinguish the light for him. He got a great kick out of it and all three of us kept our little scheme a secret. Once, the alarm clock was up and running, we set it for 6.00 a.m. every morning. When it rang, we hopped out of bed, cooked our breakfast and sat right up under the huge, bi-form optic in the middle of the lantern room. This optic was a double-decker, which meant that one optic lay on top of the other. It had five lenses to each tier, with each one having its own paraffin vapour burner. Each of these bright lamps burned two gallons of paraffin every night and emitted a brilliant, white light with intense heat, making it the warmest and brightest spot in the lighthouse. If we were in the mood for homework, we had a go at it there. Then we headed out on the cliffs with the pellet gun and aimed at the seagulls. Sometimes, we spend ages sitting on the cliff wall, looking out for shoals of mackerel.

Daddy often took us fishing, down the steep cliff, on a zig-zag path. He used a pole rod he made himself and a fishing rod he had bought for casting. Edmund and I fished with rods we made from timber. We used gut and home-made sinker weights. In summer, we caught huge amounts of pollock and mackerel. Then we salted the pollock in barrels to preserve them. After 48 hours, we took out the pollock and dried them. We made pickle with salt and a little water, just enough liquid to float a potato. We left the mackerel in a wooden tub of pickle until we wanted to eat them. Then we steeped them overnight in fresh, cold water and ate them twice a week, including every Friday, drizzled with white sauce. Our stock of mackerel always lasted right through the winter.

Edmund and I pestered Daddy to buy a boat, but he refused, saying it would only put us in danger. So, the two of us often tagged along with Pat Joe Harrington, a temporary keeper from the farm next-door, who was always in and out of the lighthouse, chatting to Daddy or helping out. Pat Joe had a small timber, fishing boat, called a punt and usually, we fished in the evening, as a lot of fish come up to feed just before dusk, when the sun has gone down and the brightness has left the water. Mainly, we used pots to catch lobster.

One evening, after lobster fishing with Pat Joe, Edmund and I decided to do some climbing. A gutter that ran around the balcony had two down-pipes, which caught rain water from the lantern and piped it down the outside of the lighthouse. We wanted to have a go at climbing up one of the pipes, to see if we could get onto the balcony and into the lighthouse. I opted to go first. I made it onto the gutter and tried to stretch my hand to reach the edge of the balcony. But I couldn't stretch far enough. I had to go back, catch onto the down-pipe and slide back down again. Edmund didn't bother trying as he knew it was a waste of time.

In the spring, Edmund and I got down to the business of painting Galley Head. We scaled up to the top of the lighthouse lantern with ease, attached to a safety harness, and painted everything white, including the balcony rails, the lantern, the dome, the sash bars on the lantern glazing and the flag mast. We whitewashed the cliff walls and courtyard walls. Having everything gleaming white improved the day mark character and ensured that the lighthouse and cliff were clearly visible to mariners during daylight hours from a long distance at sea.

Every two weeks, we vigorously cleaned and polished the lens. As a paraffin oil vapour burner was used then, the exhaust from the light blackened the lens so much that it would take us three or four hours to wipe it clean and shine it. First, we stopped the lens and faced it away from the sunlight. Then, one of us stepped inside the lens to begin the cleaning, while the other worked on the outside. Having a shining lens made all the difference to the power of the light at night, as it emitted a brighter, bigger glow.

When the oil tanks emptied, we climbed inside and washed them with buckets of water and a cloth. It was vital to keep them spotless, to stop sediment of any description making its way up to the light, as the tiniest bit of dirt could extinguish the light or set it on fire.

At Galley Head, Daddy was promoted from assistant keeper to principal keeper. This meant another move, to the principal keeper's house next door, as all the monitoring indicators and alarm systems were installed there. Edmund and I were worn out from walking over and back between the two houses, shifting all our junk.

Time was moving fast. Edmund and I left school at sixteen. In spite of all the fooling around, we both did very well in our Group Certificate and now set our sights on joining Irish Lights. But we had a number of years to fill in, as we were too young to apply.

In those gap years, I seemed to be accident prone. One evening, as Pat Joe Harrington was driving away from the Galley, I jumped up on the bonnet of his car, fell back, fractured my skull, broke my jaw and ended up unconscious. When I woke up in Bantry hospital, I saw two red lights flashing on the ceiling, like a pair of propellers. I closed my eyes to block them out. A nurse came along and said to me, 'We won't be giving you any pillow.' I thought she meant the hospital was short of pillows and I said to her, 'That's okay. I'm used to sleeping without one.'

All the doctors and nurses were polite to me and fussed over me as if I was someone special. One morning, when one of the nurses came on duty, she dashed over to me, knelt by my bedside and asked, with genuine concern in her voice, 'How are you this morning Gerry?' All of this treatment was in total contrast to my experience at school, where the teachers had always been giving out to me for clowning around.

The reeling in my head lasted for weeks, but I learned to deal with it by opening only one eye at a time and focusing on a spot on the ceiling. When the spinning finally stopped, I leaned over the bed and peeped underneath to see how it was made. In an instant, the pressure on my head came back and the spinning began again.

In the summer of 1966, Edmund and I were drawing in bales of hay with Neilie O'Donovan, on his tractor and trailer. As the tractor and empty trailer pulled out of the shed, I leaped from a stack of bales, landed on the back of the trailer, fell sideways on the ground and heard my leg snap. I roared with pain and could see that my leg was bent. Edmund rushed over and straightened it. I ended up in Bantry hospital again, had my leg set in plaster of Paris and came home on crutches. Soon, I was hopping along on the crutches, getting faster every day, until I eventually fell over and cracked the plaster. The hospital doctor was not at all pleased with me.

Once my leg mended, I began work with Matt O'Sullivan, an auctioneer in Clonakilty, while Edmund stayed farming with Neilie, milking the cows, tending to the cattle and tilling the land. By then, he had grown to love farming with a passion. When I started with Matt, he was renovating his house and teamed me up with a carpenter. We took out old windows, replaced them with new ones and fitted small kitchen units. With the revamping complete, Matt started me in the auctioneering business. I helped with the preparation for furniture auctions by cataloguing and labelling each item. Once the auction started, I had to be on full alert, as it was my job to spot the purchasers, hand them a numbered ticket and note their names and addresses for the secretary, Nellie May, then move on quickly to the next buyer. Matt's was a family-run business and after each auction we all headed to a local hotel for a meal, tired and hungry after a hard day. I became part of his family and they treated me as one of their own.

While working with Matt, Edmund and I sat the test for Irish Lights, which was set in the English language. In preparation for it, we had to brush up on the use of Morse code by lamp and semaphore, as well as English composition, maths and the geography of Ireland. Reading was also part of the exam. We needed to improve our strength as swimmers and so we began swimming lessons at the indoor swimming pool at Eglington Street in Cork.

On the night before the test, we stayed at Ward's pub in Bray, which was owned by Mammy's uncle. It was there that Mammy had accepted Daddy's proposal of marriage when he was a young, dashing assistant keeper and it was from there that they eloped to be married in Belmullet by Father Kilgallon. Little did they know then that they would raise a family of fifteen children, enough to field a football team, as my father used to say. The tale of their elopement always reminded me of a romantic story Daddy used to tell about a young assistant keeper on one of the Maidens Rocks, on the north-east, at the entrance to Larne Harbour. He fell in love with the daughter of a keeper on the other rock. When both families happened to fall out, the parents forbade the lovers to meet. The young couple eloped and rowed away to Carrickfergus on the mainland, where they married.

After sitting the exam over a period of a few days at Pembroke Street in Dublin, Edmund and I felt unsure about how we had fared. Luckily, we were called for a second test, which included communicating with ships by an international code of signals. We were also called for an interview, followed by a medical. Even though our father, uncles and grandfathers had all been lighthouse keepers, we never took it for granted that we would be accepted. We pestered Irish Lights to tell us if we would be taken, but they gave nothing away.

One winter's day, as I was chatting by the fire with Matt's sister Lelia and her son Gerard, in Lelia's house, we heard a knock on the door. It was Daddy, calling on his way to Clonakilty. 'Gerald,' he said, with a big smile on his face, 'You're called up on twelve months probation to Irish Lights and must report to the depot in Dún Laoghaire.' I nearly jumped out of my skin. Edmund was called up soon after.

At the age of nineteen, in the month of October, I bid farewell to my friends, my family and Galley Head, proud to be following in the footsteps of my father, grandfathers and uncles and thrilled to have landed the job of my dreams.

3

A Light on the Sea

The concept of the sea light was born to guide the night-time mariner safely home and avoid shipwreck. Before lighthouses were built, if a ship wanted to identify its position on the ocean, it had to sail close to the shore. Sailing ships needed a huge amount of ocean space in which to turn around and sail back out. However, sailing too close to the land often made this impossible and many marooned ships ended up on the rocks. Also, when ships experienced severe weather conditions and were near the shore, they often dropped anchor to ride out the storm. But, as their anchors and anchorages were poor, the ships regularly crashed onto the rocks. With the advent of the lighthouse, ships could locate their position at sea from a distance of twenty miles and avoid sailing too close to the land.

The first lighthouses were built by Sybian and Cushite tribes, who lived on the lower coast of Egypt. Monks and priests lived in these towers and gave instruction on sea-related matters, such as steering a ship, mapping seas and astronomy.

The first frequently-operated lighthouse was built on a headland in Troad, at Sigaeum in Greece, and came into use about 650 BC. It was considered a valuable navigational aid to ships sailing to Troy, Hellespont and the ports of Bosphorus and the Black Sea.

Built around 300 BC, the Collossus of Rhodes is known as one of the earliest lighthouses and displayed a 100-foot, bronze sculpture of Apollo at the entrance to Rhodes Harbour, holding aloft a torch, which was lit nightly. Eighty years later, an earthquake destroyed the monument.

One of the seven wonders of the ancient world, the Pharos of Alexandria, was built in 261 BC by King Ptolemy II and is considered to be the greatest lighthouse of all time. Erected 450 feet high on a 100-foot base of 'kedan' stone, with its blocks cemented together with melted lead, its open fire was visible from a distance of 29 miles. Having served 1,500 years, the tower was destroyed by an earthquake in the thirteenth century.

The Romans built many lighthouses around the coasts of Europe, usually for the dual purpose of lighting the coast and as a defence against raids by Spanish and Danish pirates. To this day, the remains of Roman lighthouses may be found along the English coast, such as at Dover Castle. At the end of the fifth century, with the demise of the Roman Empire and the onset of the Dark Ages, many of the Roman lighthouses were destroyed by pirates and invaders, until gradually the beacons were extinguished.

After the Dark Ages, especially along the French coast, the first keepers of the re-kindled lights were hermits, monks and priests. In many areas, wealthy patrons agreed to finance them on condition that they erected and tended to lighted beacons. But, their work as lighthouse keepers ended with the Dissolution of the Monasteries.

In 1536, due to a notable drop in trade, King Henry VIII granted a charter to the Guild of the Blessed Trinity on Newcastle, to design, construct and preserve lighthouses along that coastal area. He granted licenses to collect tolls and levies from passing ships, the income from which could be set against the expense of running a lighthouse. The guild operated well for two hundred years.

In 1565, under the reign of Queen Elizabeth, sea marks became subject to a preservation order. Anyone guilty of removing, altering, or destroying them was fined £100 or outlawed.

As an aid to mariners, lights were often erected on top of coastal cottages. A steel-framed basket, known as a chauffer basket, was filled with fuel, such as coal or timber, and burned all night, radiating a glow in the sky as a signal to any ship coming over the horizon that it was near land.

Dating from the Norman times of the twelfth century, Hook Point lighthouse is the oldest operational lighthouse in Ireland and the British Isles and one of the oldest in the world. Reputedly, it stands close to the site where a fifth-century Welsh monk named Saint Dubhán lit a fire beacon nightly, in an iron basket, raised on a mound of stones. The lighthouse was built with limestone and burned lime, mixed with ox's blood. Even today, traces of the blood mix can still be seen on the paintwork.

In Youghal, another Norman lighthouse was run by the sisters of Saint Anne's convent. It ceased operating during Cromwell's time and was replaced in 1852 by the present tower.

In 1665, King Charles II gave permission to Sir Robert Reading to maintain six lighthouses on the coast of Ireland: two at Howth Head and one at the Old Head of Kinsale, Barry Oge's castle near Kinsale, Hook Point and the Isle of Magee near Carrickfergus. The lighthouses were built mainly to aid mariners who traded across the channel from England to Ireland. Each lighthouse burned a coal fire on top of its roof. In 1780, a Swiss inventor named Aimé Argand invented an oil lamp and this gradually replaced the coal fire. In 1796, permission was given to build lighthouses on the coasts of Wexford, Mayo and Galway.

The coastal area from County Down to Wexford featured many hidden sunken hazards, such as sandbanks and submerged rock. These were marked with lightships, as the technology was not yet available to erect a lighthouse on them. Before the establishment of Poolbeg lighthouse, a lightship marked the entrance to the Liffey from 1732, with the Richmond becoming the first lightship to be placed in Irish open sea waters. Each lightship was fitted in the centre with a steel frame containing a lantern on top. A large, iron, mooring cable with a mushroom anchor for sandbanks, or a grab anchor for rock beds, ran up to the light vessel and kept the light moored on the station at all times. As the lightships had no means of self-propulsion, they had to be towed and anchored at each specific station.

In 1810, the Corporation for Preserving and Improving the Port of Dublin was formed and took on the responsibility for building and operating lighthouses in Ireland. Its engineer was George Halpin senior. Over a 44-year period, he oversaw the construction and establishment of fifty three new lighthouses and the modernisation and rebuilding of 15 others, as well as the introduction of many new aids to navigation, such as buoys, beacons and perches. After his death in 1854, he was succeeded by his son George junior. In 1867, the corporation's double remit – Dublin Port and the Commissioners of Irish Lights, or Irish Lights as it became known – was split into two independent corporate entities, with Irish Lights holding the responsibility for managing the coastal lights and overseeing the aids to navigation provided by county councils and port authorities. Originally, lightkeepers made contact with a ship or the mainland by semaphore, using flags, bats or lamps.

The French pioneered lighthouse optic technology and displayed their equipment at famous exhibitions in Paris. The optic is a complete unit, made up of one or more lens panels. Most of the Irish lighthouses operated with a light in the centre of a revolving lens designed in the early 1820s by a French physicist, Augustin-Jean Fresnel. In contrast to bulky lenses, the thin, large, flat, Fresnel lens captured more oblique light from a light source and made lighthouses visible from much greater distances. The semi-sphere lenses consisted of numerous circles of glass, all cut out from the same sphere and then set back into each other, but retaining the full magnification power of an uncut semi-sphere.

Each section of the semi-sphere flashed a column of light on the ocean. As the optic rotated, these spokes of light swept across the sea. The large optics floated in a bath of mercury and needed very little energy for rotation, as mercury can support thirty six times the weight that water can and is almost frictionless. Similar to the workings of a grandfather clock, the optic was rotated by a weight suspended on a steel wire rope, which descended down through a hollow, cast-iron column in the centre of the tower. At its top end, the wire rope was wound around a drum within the body of a geared timing machine and the timing machine was coupled to the optic's turning table by a drive shaft. The keeper on night watch had to wind the steel rope up a number of times every hour. The timing machine controlled the speed of the weight going down through the lighthouse and was able to develop an individual character for the station.

Most of the lighthouses around the Irish coast were built in the nineteenth century, with over sixty Irish lighthouses being built during the period of 1830 to 1863. When purchasing land for lighthouses, Irish Lights usually purchased two acres or more, to allow the keepers to be self-sufficient. The way in which certain sites were valued prior to being purchased by Irish Lights is interesting. For example, Skellig Michael boasted a massive puffin population and the sale price of the site was based on the amount of puffin feathers that could be collected every year, as puffin feathers were in much demand for pillows and fetched a high price. Other sites were valued by the amount of available seaweed, as seaweed was a valuable fertiliser.

Each lighthouse had its own individual colour scheme, known as the station's daymark character, which was recorded in 'The Admiralty List of Lights' and helped mariners identify their position at sea in daylight.

The source of light being used in lighthouses around Ireland changed many times, until finally, in the early 1900s, coal gas and oil were replaced by paraffin-oil vapour burners. From the 1960s onwards, paraffin vapour burning lights were replaced by electric bulbs. A gearless drive motor, which is a special type of motor capable of rotating at a very slow, constant speed, was used to rotate the optic.

During periods of dense fog, the ray from the lighthouse was either obscured or greatly reduced. Back in the 1700s, bells were used as fog signals. However, with the arrival of steam ships, the bell sound became less effective, as it was drowned out by the sound from the ships' engines. In the 1860s, canon guns, which let off an explosive sound, and machine-operated sirens were introduced. In time, the canon gun was replaced by tonite explosive signals and the siren by the diaphone. In contrast to gelignite, which goes for the greatest resistance when exploded, tonite goes for the least resistance, which is the atmosphere. As a result, it proved very useful as a sound signal. Each lighthouse developed its own fog signal character and this information was also included in the navigation charts.

In 1838, after a ferocious storm in February wreaked havoc from Gibraltar to the north of Scotland, a Scotsman named Thomas Drummond wrote to Irish Lights to ask if they kept weather records. As a result, all lighthouses were issued with barometers, thermometers and rain gauges and lighthouse keepers became the first meteorologists in Ireland. Later, after the Irish Meteorological Service was set up in 1936, with its headquarters at Saint Andrew's Street in Dublin, it regularly requested Irish Lights' past records. During the Troubles, or political violence of the 1920s in Ireland, the IRA raided lighthouses for anything of use, such as Morse lamps, telescopes, binoculars, batteries, paraffin oil and explosives. On 21 May 1920, they robbed Mizen Head of most of its explosives. On 20 June 1921, they seized 400 charges of cotton powder, 1,000 detonators, a telescope and binoculars from Fastnet Rock lighthouse. On 27 June 1921, the British admiralty issued a warning that fog signals on Fastnet Rock, Bull Rock and Skellig Michael were not to be relied upon, because of IRA raids on these stations. As the government failed to offer protection to the stations, Irish Lights temporarily withdrew explosive fog signals from stations around the coast, with the fog signal at Mizen Head not being re-established until 29 February 1924. At Mine Head, batteries, binoculars, a telescope, paints, oils, Morse lamps and a keeper's bicycle were stolen, while every single item was taken from Power Head, which was only a fog station. In April 1923, fourteen detonators, and two cotton powder charges were taken from Hook Point, much to the surprise of Irish Lights, who believed that Hook Point had used up all its supplies. Yet, apart from the raids and the withdrawal of fog signals, Irish Lights remained unaffected by the partition of Ireland, as politics and religion never featured in its operation. Interestingly, it stood as the only statutory body to survive the partition of Ireland.

Up until about 1969, when helicopters came into use, off-shore lighthouses used a landing derrick, or hoist, for landing stores, as well as for landing keepers and taking them off the cliff. The derrick resembled a crane and was operated manually. A large, steel spar was hinged at the base and suspended by a cable on top, which swung in a circular motion. As a boat coming to a rock to drop off a keeper and bring another ashore would have been unable to sail close enough for a step-out landing, a keeper on the rock would float a manila rope in the water. As the boat approached the rock, a crew member picked up the rope. Then, the keeper lowered a circular, timber seat, with a rope up through its centre, down from the derrick to the boat. The oncoming keeper sat on the seat and the keeper on the rock hoisted him up out of the boat, and swung the derrick over and up onto a landing stage, about 50 feet high. A keeper going ashore sat on the same seat and was swung out over the sea and lowered down until he was just above the highest wave. Then, the boat came in underneath and, as the wave lifted the boat up, a crew member grabbed the keeper, who immediately let go of the rope and fell into the boat. Once the wave cascaded, the boat pulled away from the derrick. For nearly one hundred and fifty years, Irish Lights hoisted people by derrick on and off the rock stations, including lighthouse children seated on a parent's lap, without any loss of life.

All the services provided by Irish Lights are financed out of the General Lighthouse Fund, or GLF, the income of which is derived mainly from light dues from commercial shipping at ports in Ireland and the United Kingdom, through a user-pay system, the cost of which is determined by a ship's tonnage. The Irish levies are collected by customs officials when the ships dock at ports and the charges are pooled in the Board of Trade in London, along with the dues from English Lights and Northern Lights. Since the 1920s, this income was supplemented by an annual contribution from the Irish government towards the cost of the service provided by Irish Lights in the Republic of Ireland. Annually, Irish Lights estimate the expenses for the coming year and its running costs are paid out of the GLF. Irish Lights never levied pleasure craft or fishing vessels, but the opposite was true for other countries. The huge volume of shipping sailing up and down the Thames in London meant that the levy pool was extremely well funded and consequently guaranteed that the maintenance of lighthouses down through the years was always of an extraordinarily high standard. As lighthouses were exposed to the most extreme of weather conditions, their upkeep was vital. More than a century and a half later, these buildings are still in tip-top condition and stand as proof of the excellent maintenance they always received.

From the 1800s, Irish Lights provided the families of light-keepers with good living accommodation, free of charge. Families accompanied the keeper to land, island and rock lighthouses. All unmarried keepers were encouraged to be accompanied by a female relative, to share the domestic duties and ensure the well-being of the keeper. In the 1800s, the whole family played a part in watch keeping. From 1862, if a lighthouse was undermanned, for one reason or another, and the assistance of a female family member was required, then the female assistant became employed as a female assistant keeper, or FAK. For lightkeepers and women living at isolated lighthouses, it was essential to be well-up on child delivery and medical remedies. Irish Lights provided medicines, as well as instruction on their use.

Often, lightkeepers and their families found themselves in great danger, particularly during stormy weather. In 1895, Lizzie Ryan, who lived with her brother Tom, at Eagle Island East lighthouse, where he served as an assistant keeper, wrote a letter to her mother Mary at Fastnet shore dwellings, describing a recent, terrifying storm: 'It was blowing hard all night, we went to bed at eleven that night. Polly and I never closed an eye with terror. Well at 2.30 a.m. an awful sea struck the roof bashing it and the hall door in. The first sea was dreadful. I jumped out of bed screaming. Oh God, the house is carried away. I met Tom in the hall trying to shut the back door. We were knee deep in the sea this time.'

Usually, a keeper was stationed at a particular lighthouse for about three years and was then transferred. Such a policy gave each keeper an equal chance of working at both a remote and more accessible location, and facilitated the promotion process.

Houses provided for lightkeeper families were spacious, with a slate roof, and built to the highest standard. Dwellings came fully furnished, with only the best of everything, such as good quality pine dressers and tables and top-quality linoleum. Irish Lights also supplied generous amounts of coal and household goods, such as mops, pots, pans, kettles, detergents, paints, cutlery, and crockery bearing the crest and motto of Irish Lights, '*In Salutem Omnium*', which means, 'For the safety of all'. Along with the lighthouses, all lighthouse dwellings were inspected annually by Irish Lights to ensure their maintenance. If families lived in isolated areas and had no transport of their own, a market car or taxi was provided to take them shopping, or to church on Sundays.

As many lighthouse stations had difficulty in obtaining a fresh supply of milk, lightkeepers were encouraged to keep goats, where practicable. Being sure-footed even on steep ground, goats were considered ideal for a cliff-top location.

In the local community, the keeper was held in high esteem, especially as he and his family brought a welcome boost to local business and also because he could calculate numbers, read and write. Regularly, he was asked to write a letter for locals who wanted to contact relatives abroad. Also, romance often blossomed and many of the keepers married local girls.

Normally, the keeper taught his own children at the lighthouse or employed a tutor for part of the year. However, to comply with the school act of the late 1800s, which stipulated that all children attend primary school, Irish Lights built shore dwellings for the keepers' families who would have previously lived with the keeper on rock or isolated island lighthouses. As a result, stations where the keeper no longer lived continuously became relieving stations. Also, to allow each keeper regular time ashore with his family, additional manpower was required and so the stations usually employed three or four keepers, working in shifts of four hours on and eight hours off, except when there was fog, tender deliveries or if a tradesman needed assistance.

The lightkeeper's job was pensionable. Prior to retirement, keepers and their wives were often sent to one-keeper lighthouses, such as Greencore, Howth East Pier, Duncannon and Youghal, as one-keeper stations were comfortable and conveniently located. Once a lightkeeper retired from Irish Lights, he had to seek other accommodation for himself and his family. During the 1960s, Irish Lights encouraged keepers to purchase homes for themselves and helped them secure a mortgage. In the 1980s, a small charge was imposed on those living in lighthouse properties, due to legal reasons

By the time I joined Irish Lights in 1969, Ireland had 80 manned lighthouses dotted all around its coast. Like my father, grandfathers and uncles before me, I would serve at many of these stations and experience the isolation, camaraderie, thrills, triumphs, tragedies and dangers of life as a lighthouse keeper. Yet, while my new career would discipline me to a certain degree, it would fail to quell my quest for risk and adventure. This pursuit, so prevalent since my childhood, would bring me to the brink of death many times, especially during my training.

4

A Keeper in the Making

At the lighthouse depot in Dún Laoghaire, I collected my bed bag, which was a stiff, green bag, made of sail canvas, with a stitched, hinged cover secured with a pull cord, and lined with PVC material to keep the contents dry. It contained all my bed clothes: a pillow; linen pillow cover; two linen sheets; three Foxford Woolen Mills blankets; and a mattress cover made of rough fabric. Then, I headed for the Baily lighthouse on the hill at Howth Head, on the north coast of Dublin Bay, as this was the base for all the supernumeraries, or trainee lightkeepers. The Baily light guided ships in and out of the port of Dublin and stood as a familiar landmark to ships sailing along the east coast.

At the time, 30 supernumeraries were on the books at the station, all coming and going at different times. The lighthouse had bunk beds for about 12. When the numbers swelled, some of us slept on the floor. All of us shared the food and ordered our supplies by phoning Kitty in Gaffneys' shop at the top of the hill. The Gaffneys also ran a pub and restaurant, and we went there for lunch most days. Whenever we did decide to cook, there was always plenty of messing about, with tossed pancakes usually landing on the floor and eggs being thrown from one to the other with gusto.

Mainly, training consisted of learning basic skills on the job. The principal keeper instructed us on dismantling and reassembling the paraffin vapour burner, which was a bright, treble-50

41

millimetre regenerative burner, with three mantles on top – the largest paraffin burner used in lighthouses and consuming about six gallons of paraffin each night. Paraffin oil was delivered up through the centre of the burner and some oil was diverted to heat retorts, which were gun metal tubes with a very fine nipple on top and were kept constantly hot by small flame burners. The pressurised, heated paraffin oil in the retorts turned to vapour, which in turn changed to gas. The gas spread out into the three mantles and these emitted a brilliant white glow.

At two million candelas, the Baily light was one of the most powerful on the Irish coast. Its double bull's-eye lens panels magnified the light to this level and gave it a distinctive flashing character. Because of the optic's massive weight, it floated in a bath of mercury. Its timing machine powered by the standard weights was capable of rotating the optic. The timing machine had to be wound every forty minutes.

We learned how to operate a fog signal, which at the Baily was called a diaphone. It gave off a loud, droning sound, like a bull in agony, and was activated by compressed air, which was pumped in huge volumes to a pressure of about 30 pounds per square inch, the same pressure that we pump into a car tyre. The volume was colossal.

To start up the fog signal, we used two horizontal, single cylinder engines, made by Ruston and Hornsby. We started the engines' fly wheels with compressed air. We opened the valves and allowed the air in at a pressure of about 300 pounds. The surge of air drove the cylinder back and the engines began to rotate. Often, they proved temperamental and tried our patience, as they took time to kick in and pick up pace.

Once the engines were underway and connected to large pumps, they were capable of delivering a massive amount of air. All the air was stored in two large air receivers measuring about four feet in diameter and 15 feet in length. We opened the exhaust valves on these receivers and the air inlet to the fog horn. The fog horn blasted off from its own timing mechanism, which was permanently set. The engines needed a constant watch, as they had to be oiled frequently. When the fog cleared, we stopped the engines. Because of the giant fly wheel, we were able to use the engines as a pump to backfill our compressed air bottles for starting up the next time.

The radio-telephone at the Baily was the hub for all messages being sent to and from Irish Lights, as well as from all lifeboats at sea to the various honorary secretaries. The principal keeper instructed us on the use of the marine radios, for which we had to be certified with a radio licence. We practised radio communication with off-shore lighthouses, such as Tuskar Rock off the Wexford coast, and Mew Island off Belfast, as off-shore lighthouses had no telephones then and could only make contact by radio. The VHF frequency ranged between 30 and 50 miles, while the Medium frequency ranged up to 150 miles, depending on the weather. If we needed to contact our head office in Dublin, for example to request an extra keeper if one of our keepers took ill, we used our own in-house alphabetic code. If a vessel was sinking and unable to make contact, we sent off a May Day Relay on its behalf. A May Day Relay is a call for help for a capsized boat and the message begins by repeating the words May Day Relay three times. When we issued a May Day Relay from the Baily, it reached every ship within range, from Wexford to Belfast and over to the Welsh coast. We described the capsized boat and gave its position in relation to the lighthouse. We also contacted Dún Laoghaire Lifeboat or Howth Lifeboat and directed them to the casualty. We continued our radio watch by keeping in constant radio communication with the lifeboats until the rescue was complete. Then, we finished our transmission with the words, 'Baily listening out'.

Under the supervision of the principal keeper, we practised Morse code, semaphore and the international code of signals, which we learned off by heart from a booklet entitled 'Brown's Signal Reminder'. Every lighthouse keeper received the booklet on joining Irish Lights. From the manual, we learned the corresponding flag mast colours for each letter of the alphabet. For example, the letter 'A' is represented by a white and blue flag, with the white colour to the mast and the blue colour flying. If the flag is flown on its own, it means a ship has a diver down underneath the vessel. Use of the international code of signals makes it possible to communicate with all mariners, regardless of language.

We also learned how to use ropes for rigging derricks, for landing equipment safely onto a rock and for tying up a boat. We were taught how to splice ropes and steel wire, as well as how to make an eye on the end. We became skilled at making an array of knots, such as the clove hitch, rolling hitch, carrick bend and reef knot. We practised these loops, as well as everything else that we learned at the Baily, over and over again at the lighthouses to which we were assigned during the probation and training period.

At night, the senior trainees filled us with tales about certain principal keepers around the coast who were sure to make our lives hell if we were unlucky enough to be landed at one of their stations, which was all a load of guff. But, they managed to put the fear of god into some of the lads, especially guys from the inland, who had no idea what to expect.

After weeks of training at the Baily, I was sent on relief duty to Wicklow Head lighthouse, south of Wicklow town. There, I learned about the running of the station and the different type of lighting equipment used, which was much smaller than that used at the Baily, as Wicklow Head didn't need as strong a light range, due to the lightships moored on the sandbanks off shore. My abiding memory of my time there is the sound of the seals, moaning and groaning.

Having done my stint at Wicklow Head, I returned to the Baily, where I was instructed to go for a fortnight to Inishtearaght – a rock station completed in 1869, off the south-west coast of Ireland, on the outer of the Blasket Islands in County Kerry, on the most westerly part of Europe, with a peak of about 700 feet above sea level. From the outset, Irish Lights encouraged the keeping of goats on the rock. Sadly, in 1913, one of the keepers plunged to his death while rounding up the goats for milking.

My father had worked as an SAK on Inishtearaght. One fine day, he dived off the landing for a swim. When he surfaced, he found himself beside a basking shark. He got the fright of his life and swam back to the landing as fast as he could. But he need not have panicked, as the shark sucked plankton, which meant he was not dangerous. From listening to my father talking about Inishtearaght, I knew that one of the jobs most dreaded by keepers was greasing the cables of the aerial hoist, especially in the bitter cold of winter.

Inishtearaght would be my first rock station and I had to prepare a grub order to last me two weeks. I telephoned my order to McCarthy's shop in Castletownbere. The food was arranged in a labelled basket and sent to the newly-constructed, nearby helicopter base. After travelling down from Dublin by train, I booked into a local bed and breakfast house. On the following morning, a mini bus collected me, along with other keepers heading for stations on the south-west coast, and drove us to the Roancarrig dwellings, where I had lived as a child and where the helicopter base was located. I felt chuffed that I would be flying to Inishtearaght by helicopter, especially as I would be on board the first ever helicopter flight to the rock station, as before that all landings to Inishtearaght had been made by ship. I gathered up all the baskets marked for Inishtearaght and double checked that I had all the provisions, as I was responsible for collecting all the orders for the station, including those of the other two keepers already on the rock. At that time, lighthouses always had three keepers on the stations, with each keeper working eight hours out of 24, usually in one-man shifts of four hours, to provide a round-the-clock watch.

That flight to Inishtearaght was the trip of a lifetime for me. All through the journey, I marvelled at the speed of the helicopter and revelled in the verve of its vibrations as it fought its way through the updraft. We flew high above the mountains, soaring over the coastline, on past Waterville and Valentia. Then, as we neared Inishtearaght, the high, jagged-rock station came into view. I spotted the helicopter pad below, which was located three-quarter ways up the steep rock. It seemed tiny. Landing a helicopter on Inishtearaght wasn't easy, especially because of the height of the rock, the location of the pad and the air turbulence. The helicopter had to descend almost directly onto the pad. It was the only way.

Once I stepped out of the helicopter, I immediately sensed the isolation of the rock, which was surrounded only by the swirling Atlantic Ocean. Having grown up as the son of a lightkeeper, I was well aware that working on a rock station meant being stranded on a cliff top. But I knew I could detach myself from all the luxuries of shore life and live only for the present. My main feeling was one of anticipation, as I was eager to explore every inch of the rock.

After meeting the acting principal keeper Aidan Polly, and the assistant keeper Séamus Flaherty from the Aran Islands, I headed out on my own for the rocks, impatient to scour the cliff. It was a haven for birds, among them fulmars, kittiwakes, herring gulls, razorbills, great black-backed gulls, lesser black-backed gulls and thousands of puffins. The cliff was infested with rabbits, including a lot of black rabbits. The rabbits on the cliff had never been struck with myxomatosis – the disease introduced to Ireland in 1954 by the government to cut down on the rabbit population, as farmers had been complaining that the animals were destroying their crops - and so, the rabbits on Inishtearaght had multiplied over and over again. The cliff had much loose soil, which suited the rabbits for burrowing. The keepers never snared them for food.

During my two weeks on Inishtearaght, I learned much about its fog signal, which was similar to that at the Baily, but operated by a more modern engine. The light apparatus also differed slightly, but soon became familiar to me, as only two forms of light were used in the lighthouses – a triple mantle or a single mantle light. Also, I put in a lot of radio practice, as we had two radios, one for helicopter use and the other for our own lighthouse use.

Watch keeping at Inishtearaght consisted of a light watch at night and also a fog watch. If visibility closed in to less than three miles, we started a fog signal. We took our marks, or points of reference, from Inishvickillane – a nearby island owned by Charles Haughey – or if it was dark at night, we made a judgement from the rays of light, as they reflected any density of fog. The first light night watch on Inishtearaght started at 6.00 p.m. and ended at 10.00 p.m., with only one keeper on watch at a time, as was the norm on every lighthouse. Each watch lasted four hours. At that time, coastal shipping around Inishtearaght consisted mainly of oil tankers sailing between Foynes and Milford Haven, with some traffic sailing from America, usually trade ships heading for Cobh, England and other parts of Europe.

Once, when a thick fog descended over Inishtearaght, it lingered for three full days. We kept the fog engines running constantly and blasted the fog horn non-stop. I became so used to the drone of the engines and the moan of the fog horn that I took no notice. When the fog finally cleared, I couldn't sleep because of the quietness. Now, I could hear clearly the squawking of the seagulls on the rock. Up until then, I had never noticed their wailing.

While on Inishtearaght, I tended to the vegetable garden. I remembered that an archaeologist once told me that Skellig Michael and Inishtearaght had never been covered in ice during the

Ice Age and, as a result, both rocks were dotted with vegetation pockets of soil.

When the Irish Lights' tender ship *Ierne* landed barrels of paraffin oil or diesel, we hauled them up the rock by using the carriage system, which ran on a sloped tramway. Due to the number of steps and steep incline, it was impossible to carry anything all the way up the cliff from the boat landing, apart from something that was light enough to be taken in one hand. To operate the carriage, we had to start the fog signal compressors. We used an air winch, with a steel cable, to lower a platform all the way down to the landing, and then hoist it up again. The platform had small, track wheels and ran on a tramway system. Then, we pumped the oil into our storage tanks.

When the *Ierne* sailed to Inishtearaght with building materials or storage goods, we used an aerial hoist to bring them up the cliff. The hoist was made of a steel cable and anchored high over the landing. The cable stretched from a platform above the store room in the middle of the cliff, high over the boat landing, across the mouth of the cove. It was anchored into the finger of protruding rock, on the far-off side of the cove. The lighthouse tender launched its motor boat and rowing boat, or cutter as it was known, unloaded the goods onto it and sailed in near the cliff for us to begin the hoist.

Originally, Inishtearaght had two semi-detached houses, identical to those at Galley Head. But in the 1900s, when the lightkeepers' families moved ashore to Valentia, the upstairs of one of the houses was removed and the lower storey was converted into an engine room for generators and compressors for fog signals. The other house was used to accommodate keepers, with each keeper having his own bedroom and sharing a kitchen and living room area.

My memory of the kitchen and living room at Inishtearaght is that it was like living inside a radio, as it was a mass of wires, with cables flying over and back in all directions. Aerials for our two radios were connected through a special insulating unit on the window that ran up the cliff. We had a range for cooking and also for heating. I found myself checking the water to make sure it was safe to drink. I spilled a drop from the water tank onto the hot range to test it, just as my father had done during my stay with him on Ballycotton Island when I was a child.

When it came to meal times, all three keepers ate together. Aidan Polly did all the cooking and that suited me fine, as I hated cooking. Every day, I ate a full loaf of white bread. As the days went by, the colour of the bread changed. It grew a beard of fungus and became as hard as plywood. But I still ate it. We stored the bread in our lockers, which were infested with little mites. These little mites made a holiday home of our bread. Before we cut a slice of bread, we hammered the loaf off the table first. The little devils scattered and ran for their lives. A sample of the mites was later sent off to UCC, to check if they were safe to eat. It was found that they were totally harmless, which kept our spirits up no end! In time to come, when I'd had my fill of stale white bread and couldn't stomach it any longer, I mastered the art of making brown bread, as my mother gave me her recipe, showed me how to mix the ingredients and taught me how to knead dough until the cracks disappeared. Later, the arrival of deep freezers meant better food for the keepers.

At that time, Inishtearaght kept three goats on the rock, including one goat that gave milk. I loved drinking the goat's milk, as I had acquired a taste for it from my time spent with my father on Ballycotton lighthouse. We milked the goat daily.

Aidan Polly's ability to make rum fascinated me. I watched him as he securely fitted a vegetable marrow on top of a sweet jar, so that the air could not get in or out. He cleared out all the core of the marrow, bored a few holes in the bottom of the vegetable, cut the top off to scoop out the centre seeds and filled the hole with a mixture of raisins and sugar. Then, he replaced the cap of the marrow, sealed it up with insulation tape and left it sit there for almost two weeks. It gave off a strong whiff of alcohol and the scent grew stronger as the days went by. When it was time for him to go ashore, he had a nice bottle of rum to take home.

During my leisure time, I read a lot. It was impossible not to read, as the station stored a wealth of reading material, including stacks of books left behind by past lightkeepers and a Carnegie library, which was a collection of books stored in a small, wooden cabinet with two doors and the word 'Carnegie' written in front. Carnegie libraries were created with money donated by the Scottish-American businessman and philanthropist Andrew Carnegie. Under the grant scheme, more than 2,000 libraries were set up all over the world, including the United States, Britain, Canada, Australia, New Zealand, Serbia, Caribbean, Fiji and Ireland, many of them for public use, and some located in universities. Between 1883 and 1929, Britain and Ireland together received funding for over six hundred of these libraries.

Sometimes, I scoured through old visitors' books, showing pages of the signatures of anyone who visited the lighthouse, such as teachers who came from the Great Blasket Island to do projects with the children of the keepers, when families lived on the rock. Some of the teachers visited every few months, or when the weather allowed. Strangely, most of the women who had signed the book were called Kate. I watched television too, on an old, rented, black-and-white set. While the reception was good, the television set was brutal. To keep it working, we had to make sure the buttons were jammed in constantly. But my greatest joy was climbing and exploring the cliff, even though it was late November and many of the birds had long flown to warmer climates.

One morning, when I came across scraps of metal in the workshop, I decided to erect a weather vane at the top of Inishtearaght. I set off to climb its peak, 700 feet above sea level, with the metal, wires, ropes for rigging and a bag of cement, all strapped to my back. When I reached the top, I put up the vane, bedded it into the rock and anchored four stays to the ground to hold it in position once the cement hardened. It stayed in place and worked well for ten years, giving helicopter pilots a true wind indication.

When my two weeks on Inishtearaght ended, I felt excited to be leaving, simply because I was thrilled at the thought of another helicopter ride. After coming ashore, I popped in to McCarthy's shop in Castletownbere to pay for my basket of food. The care and attention with which the women in the shop prepared the food for the keepers never failed to amaze me, because they always arranged the baskets as if they were doing it for one of their own. Then, I headed back to base at the Baily. Now, for the first time since joining Irish Lights, I felt like one of the lads.

From then on, over the next year, I came and went between the Baily and other lighthouses, doing stints of relief duty all over the coast, usually standing in for a keeper on sick leave, then returning to the Baily for a spell, until I was given instructions on my next station.

My next posting was to the forbidding Fastnet Rock – the most famous lighthouse in Ireland, mainly because it stands as the midpoint in the renowned, classic, offshore Fastnet yachting race. Its character of light was one white flash every five seconds, with a range of light of about 27 nautical miles.

Built of Cornish granite blocks in 1897 on the most southerly part of Ireland, off-shore from Crookhaven in County Cork and towering 160 feet above sea level, Fastnet Rock was known as Ireland's teardrop, as it was the last part of Ireland that nineteenth century emigrants saw as they sailed to America. Deep water surrounds the jagged rock and powerful currents encircle it, making a landing by boat almost impossible, especially during spring tides. Heavy fogs plague its coast and reduce visibility to an arm's length.

When I arrived on Fastnet by helicopter, I placed all my belongings and the food baskets in a crate and helped winch them up by rope to the kitchen at the top of the tower, which had eight flights of stairs, with at least seventeen steps on each flight. As I approached the lighthouse door at the bottom, I felt intimidated by the vastness and height of the tower, an elegant finger of granite, pointing high into the sky. Even though I had heard about Fastnet all through my childhood, my mental image came nowhere near what I was seeing and I looked up in awe, overwhelmed by its tall, majestic stature.

Considered to be the quintessential tower lighthouse, the present tower was completed on 27 June 1904. Designed by William Douglass and built under the supervision of James Kavanagh – who lived and worked on the rock continuously for ten to twelve months of every year, for almost seven years – it brought the art of masonry construction to the pinnacle of perfection.

Once I went inside the door, I realised it was just like any other lighthouse, with winding flights of stairs and handrails. But the noise was deafening, as all the electric generators were stored inside on the second flight, unlike at Inishtearaght, where they were outside. The droning was constant, almost wearing.

The kitchen was located right under the lantern and a steel weight trunk, used originally to run the machines for driving the lenses, ran right down through its centre. It was the hub of activity, as all radio communication was made from there. It served as a functional area, had no comforts and was very congested, mainly because it stored a huge, slate water tank. A gutter on an outside balcony collected the water and piped it into the kitchen. This water was used only for washing purposes, never for consumption, as it contained a good deal of sea spray. The kitchen had three windows, with massive panoramic views.

Once I'd seen the entire lighthouse, I headed off out alone to explore the rock. I climbed down steps leading to a platform and continued on to the bottom of the cliff. As I stood there, a huge wave struck the rock and rose up 20 feet over me. But I was lucky, because the tower sheltered me. I clutched the handrail tightly and held on for dear life until the wave died down. Then I rushed back up the cliff, with my senses on the alert, fully aware that I was now on the hazardous Fastnet rock. That was my eye-opener and from then on I viewed the Fastnet as an extremely dangerous place. The rock was a very different place to Galley Head, where I had grown up, as the force of the waves at Galley Head never mounted so high. Now, I believed and understood all I had heard about Fastnet as a child.

All through my childhood, I had overheard many lightkeepers say that Fastnet swayed to and fro, three feet at either side of the centre, at the top of the light, as it had been deliberately built in a particular way to allow a certain amount of flexibility, without harming the tower. Otherwise, the lighthouse would snap in two due to the vast amount of water that whipped up over the tower, as well as the power and the speed at which the sea travelled. Also, storms around Fastnet can easily shift 20-ton weights or rip rocks of that size into the sea.

With its skirt-line, bell-cast design, the tower flares out at the bottom, as well as at the level of the balcony, to throw the sea away from the lantern. Each stone of the lighthouse is dovetailed into all neighbouring stones, making the tower a monolith, or single-stone structure. As a result, the tower is very safe, as it would be impossible to remove any stone without stripping it from the top down, unlike the first lighthouse at Fastnet.

Made of flanged, thick cast-iron plates and bolted onto the top of the rock with two-foot bolts, the first tower was built at Fastnet in 1854. A similar lighthouse on the nearby Calf Rock, off Dursey Island, was whipped away by a ferocious storm after it snapped in two on 26 November 1881, proving yet again that the mighty force of the sea cannot be beaten; only contained. Luckily all six inhabitants survived and were finally rescued by Dursey Island boatmen, after being marooned in the kitchen of the dwelling for days. In the same gale, the Fastnet lantern was smashed and one lens was considerably damaged. Fears increased for the safety of Fastnet and it was decided to dismantle the cast-iron tower and build a new lighthouse, with the sealed-off base of the original being retained as an oil store for the new station.

Fastnet boasts a unique central heating system. Its generator engines are water-cooled. Instead of letting heated water go to waste, it is piped throughout the tower and through radiators, to cool the water before re-circulating it back through the engines.

The sea rushes at Fastnet in a westerly wind. About a half mile west of Fastnet, a sunken rock, or ledge, breaks the gushing waves at a height of about 90 feet, chopping off their top, as they thrash their way towards Fastnet at 50 miles an hour, or more. When the first of the rapid waves batter against the lighthouse, they trap pockets of air. Then, as the waves move quickly over them, the pockets of air become compressed and explode, releasing their energy into the waves, giving the waves that extra lift and heeling them right over the top of the tower.

One night, I was sitting in the kitchen watching television when I heard a huge explosion. The television picture disappeared and I felt a strange sensation of movement, as if I was sitting on a rubber chair. I said to one of the lightkeepers, 'What is wrong with this chair? It's just like a piece of rubber.' He told me that the tower was shaking and explained that when a massive wave crashed into the bottom of the tower, the water rushed up over the top of the lighthouse. Its pressure shook the tower, forced water up through the waste pipe in the kitchen and into the kitchen sink, and blanked the television. Once the wave collapsed, the television picture returned. To stop the wave breaking into the sink, we used to fill the sink up half-way with water and stand a saucepan of water on the stopper. In times of storm, the shaking would continue until the storm died down, which meant it would sway for a period of about ten hours.

To protect itself against stormy conditions, the Fastnet had gun-metal window storm shutters, built into the same curvature as the lighthouse. Each window was fitted with a small pane of thick, storm glazing. As a result, only a limited amount of light shone through and any water that hit the panes was instantly dumped.

Situated on the flight above the kitchen, the service room stored all the mechanism for revolving the lens and the pedestal on which the lens stood. The room had access to the upper balcony, from which we lowered the firing jib for the fog signal and hung on the explosive charge. After coming back inside the lighthouse, we winched the firing jib up in the air, well clear of the lighthouse. Then, every few minutes, when the alarm bell rang to signal the sequence, we fired. Sometimes, it was too dangerous to stand on the balcony, as it was all too easy to be washed away by gigantic waves, surging up the tower, especially in winter.

One vicious, stormy, winter's night, stones rolled on the ocean floor and clattered against the tower. One of them crashed into one of the storm shutters and burst in the window. Then, huge waves gushed through and knocked the generators out of order. As a result, we replaced the storm glazing in the engine room with sheets of brass.

Any time the weather turned for the worst and the sea whipped high over the tower, I'd see the fear in the eyes of Jim, the principal keeper, but he never voiced his terror. Often, in calmer conditions, he'd stand on the balcony, motionless, gazing far out to sea, lost in his thoughts, as if he was carrying the world on his shoulders or visiting some dark corner of his mind, totally cut off from myself and the other keeper, alone in a world of his own.

I spent my first Christmas away from home on Fastnet. To celebrate, I had included a cake, a pudding and a chicken in my provisions. Christmas was the only time of year that the lighthouses relaxed the routine about alcohol. But that made no difference to me, as I wasn't a drinker.

Around tea time on Christmas eve, the other keepers drank a few bottles of stout and we sat around the kitchen chatting. We reminisced too and exchanged stories, such as the one about the so-called miracle at Inishowen, when an old man in a wheelchair, on hearing the sound of a fog horn for the first time, became convinced it was the moaning of a sea monster, jumped out of his wheelchair and ran for his life.

The seasonal tale about the geese of Tommy Lawlor, principal keeper on Inishowen, was another favourite. Tommy had two geese to fatten for Christmas and kept them with his hens in the big garden near the west light. Shortly before Christmas, Tommy and his family went on holiday, leaving the remaining three keepers in charge of the fowl. After feeding the fowl one morning, one of the keepers forgot to close the garden gate. The hens and geese escaped and, in the panic to round them up, Tommy's two geese waddled down the steps to the boat landing, were washed into the water, whisked up-river with the flood tide and landed at Greencastle, where they were caught by a man with a big family and ended up on his table for Christmas dinner.

Then, we had the story about Brendan McMahon, an acting principal keeper on the Skelligs, who needed to unblock the earth closet of a small building close to the tower, while the principal keeper was on leave. Brendan had the bright idea of detonating the fog signal charges buried in the choked drain. But he got more than he bargained for when the explosion blew off most of the slates on the roof. He watched in disbelief as they smashed to bits on Seal Cove, 170 feet below the tower, and went into a panic, knowing he would have to locate spare slates, repair the roof, shovel out the choked drain and wash down the splattered walls, all before the principal keeper returned.

Another tale was the one about the keeper who started pinching flour from his fellow keepers after using up all his own provisions. Once the principal keeper found out, he went off, got some white cement and mixed it with the flour – making sure that the keeper learned his lesson the hard way.

Of course, we got great mileage out of the yarn about the architectural technician who was sent out to survey Fastnet for the installation of showers and a flush toilet. He wasn't long landed when nature called. He headed down the rocks and carefully chose his spot. But, expecting the keepers above to spy on him, he kept peeping back up at the lighthouse as he went about his business. Convinced he hadn't been spotted, he was almost ready to climb back up the rocks when he heard a thunderous applause coming from the sea below. Shocked, he looked behind him only to see a boat-load of people clapping and cheering and letting him know that he hadn't been so discreet after all.

The story-telling went on until about 10.00 p.m., when we made radio contact with fellow keepers all over the coast, as it was traditional that colleagues sang to each other over the radio on Christmas eve, one at a time, until about 4.00 a.m. Being the non-drinker on the rock, I was able to do the necessary watches and cover the Christmas morning shift, to let the lads recover. While I was never lonely on Fastnet, I was looking forward to returning to the Baily after my four-week stint and getting out and about.

During any hours off at the Baily, I often popped into Dublin city centre, mainly to browse around the shops or go to the cinema, where I became a huge fan of all the big-screen legends, like Clint Eastwood, Henry Fonda and Kirk Douglas. I rarely went dancing. Not being very tall, I had an inferiority complex about my height – so much so that, within minutes of stepping inside the door of a ballroom, I always rushed back out again. Once, I happened to meet up with Stephen Stocker, the pal who had lived next door to us at Mine Head. He had also joined Irish Lights and we were both stationed at the Baily at the same time. We headed off to a dancehall, where Johnny McEvoy was playing. Stephen had a magical pair of eyes and could pick up a girl with only a glance. But I never seemed to have any luck.

Back at the Baily, how to get a girlfriend seemed to be the topic of every conversation for all the supernumeraries, myself included and my twin Edmund, who had joined Irish Lights only months after me. Everyone shared their own ideas and tips. Some guys said it was best to stay aloof, to play it cool, pretend not to give a toss and keep the girls guessing. Others said the only way to win a girl was to lay on the charm and spoil her rotten. Then, Edmund came up with his very own master plan.

One of Edmund's pals, another trainee, had a girlfriend in Dublin, a civil servant. When the pal was posted off to a rock lighthouse, Edmund phoned the girlfriend and pretended to be his pal. He played a blinder mimicking his voice and she fell for it. He suggested to her that she should go out with his friend Edmund Butler while he was away, reasoning that there was no point in her staying in and that Edmund needed someone to go out with. So, the two of them went off on a date. Of course, when Edmund told me the story, I decided that I should have a piece of the action too. And so we agreed that instead of Edmund turning up for the next date, I'd go along and pretend to be Edmund, as it was impossible to tell the difference between us. The timing was perfect, because by then Edmund had been posted to Ballycotton lighthouse on relief duty.

In the lead-up to the date, Edmund rang me day after day. He spent hours on the phone filling me in on all the details about the girl, such as what she looked like and where they had gone together, so that I wouldn't mess up. By the time the night of the date arrived, I felt cock-sure I knew her inside out.

Well before the arranged time, I turned up at the GPO, which, along with Clery's on the other side of the road, was a popular meeting place for young couples. I stood there with my back to the wall and my hands in my pockets, dressed to kill in my bell bottoms and best shirt. Every now and then, I flicked back my mad, bushy hair and patted it down. I looked to the left and right of me, keeping an eye out for her. At one stage, I spotted a girl walking towards me with a big smile on her face. Convinced it was my date, I was about to approach her when I suddenly saw, out of the corner of my eye, another girl looking at me and laughing. Immediately, I knew she was my date. She was very pretty, but much taller than I expected, as she towered above me. I strolled over, looked up at her and said casually, 'So, where will we go tonight?' I knew by her response that she didn't suspect a thing and that she thought I was Edmund.

We headed off to some musical show in the city and the more she spoke, the more I realised that Edmund had fed me a pack a lies about her and that in fact I knew absolutely nothing about the girl. At one stage, she said to me, 'By the way, I got those photos.' Of course, this meant nothing to me and all I could say was, 'Really?' But I kept my cool, played it by ear for the rest of the night and got away with it.

On our second date, her sister came along, as well as my older brother Lawrence, who was working in Customs and Excise in Dublin. The four of us met up early in the evening and went on a bus ride, spinning around the city. As the night went on, I decided that the joke was going too far, especially as Lawrence was play-acting, calling me 'Edmund' all night, with a huge smirk on his face, and trying his best to trip me up by firing a string of questions at me about our other dates. Eventually, I said to her, 'Look, I'm not myself at all. I'm somebody else.' I told her that I was out with her on the last date and that before that it was my twin brother who had taken her out. She was having none of it and the more I tried to persuade her, the more she insisted that I was having her on. Anyway, after seeing her home, I never made another date and that ended my first, brief romance.

Soon after, I was posted to Aranmore Island lighthouse, where I found plenty to occupy my mind, other than finding a girlfriend. Once I saw that the station stored sodium chlorate weed killer, I decided to make use of it. I mixed it with sugar, squeezed one end of a four-foot pipe tightly, packed in the explosive mixture, sealed up the other end and drilled a small hole for a fuse. Nearby on the island, I found an old ruin of a British coastguard's house. I buried my bomb in one of the rooms, lit the fuse, jumped out the window and ran for my life. I had run only a short distance when I heard a thunderous explosion. It resounded all over the sea but could not be heard back on the mainland, because of the lie of the land. I raced back to the ruin to check out the damage and failed to find any trace of shrapnel. I now felt like I was a qualified bomb maker, ready for action.

Wherever there was danger to be found, I was drawn to it. And my stint on Skellig Michael – a beautiful, steep, terraced, rocky island off the south-west coast of Ireland – was no different. The lighthouse itself sits on the larger of the two Skellig islands, eight miles from the mainland, off Valentia Island in County Kerry and north-east of Puffin Island. Famous world-wide, the Skelligs is one of only two UNESCO World Heritage sites in the Republic of Ireland. Once occupied by monks and dating back to pre-Christian times, it boasts an array of flora, such as sea pink and sea campion, as well as a magical treasure of beehive dwellings, oratories, crosses, wells, a chapel, and a monastery built almost at the top of the 700-foot rock. Even from the air, as the helicopter prepared to land on Skellig Michael, I could sense its danger and the lure of its jagged, almost vertical rocks, rising like Gothic churches into the sky.

While the site itself enthralled me, its population of seabirds blew my breath away, thousands of them, chirping and twittering in a deafening crescendo, among them gannets, fulmars, kittiwakes, razorbills, common guillemot, Atlantic puffin, storm petrels and manx shearwaters.

One morning, as I was climbing up from the boat landing, a bird high up on the cliff dislodged a sharp piece of rock, about the size of a dinner plate. It rolled on down on its edge, twirled directly towards me and passed right in front of my face, leaving some earth on my nose. If I had been only an inch or two further ahead, it would have buried itself in my head. On reflection of this incident and the explosion on Aranmore, I decided I was invincible.

One day, I made up my mind to climb to the peak of Skellig Michael, about 700 feet above sea level. I reached Christ's Saddle, which is where the rock divides into a turn to the right for the monastery, in which monks had resided many years previously, and to the left for the rock's summit. If I veered left, I knew I would have to pass the Eye of the Needle, which meant going through a piece of the rock and coming out on the other side. But, after turning left, I wanted to explore a different passage to the top and figured there had to be another way to the peak. So I turned right. I climbed out onto a huge lump of rock. I found it impossible to locate slots to stick my toes, as the rock was extremely sheer at nearly 90 degrees, with a drop of almost 700 feet below me. I had very little grip on the rock and could only barely hold on with my fingers. Soon, I realised I was in serious difficulty. I couldn't climb back down to Christ's Saddle and I couldn't stay in the one position for any length of time, as I had nothing sturdy to grasp. I had to keep climbing upwards. I continued on, out along this precipitous rock, getting deeper into trouble with each move. I hoped that the edge on the opposite side of the cliff might be more favourable. But it was worse, as the rock on the north-side edge was extremely smooth. I could not afford to stop and kept on climbing. I put one leg on the north side and the other on the south. Then, I squeezed my knees together and tried to hold on. I grabbed the rock above me and pulled myself up, leading with my small finger. As I repeated this movement, a piece of rock came away in my hand. I let it go, but didn't panic. My father's advice about climbing came ringing in my ears, 'Always rely on your hands and feet.' I positioned my face only about three inches from the rock to focus my concentration on each movement.

As I started to resume the climb, I spotted some people below on Christ's Saddle, all kitted out in mountaineering gear. One of them shouted up, 'Do that again.' He was referring to the falling rock, which he would have seen plunging down the cliff and shattering on rock on the water's edge. That got the wind up me. He obviously didn't realise I was in trouble. Instead of roaring for help, I shouted at him to get stuffed.

I continued struggling up the vertical edge. I kept my bottle, never gave fear a chance to take over, and focused firmly on my task until finally I reached the peak, relieved to have made it to the top. Then I climbed back down the normal way. But I kept my escapade to myself, to avoid being reprimanded.

One of my most poignant moments on the Skellig Michael was when I visited the memorial erected to Patrick and William Callaghan – two children who died and were buried on the rock in the 1860s, when their father William was stationed there as the principal lightkeeper. Both children died only four months apart. At home, I'd often heard Daddy talk about the Callaghans of the Skelligs and my brother Lawrence had met some of their descendants. At the time of the boys' deaths, Mr Callaghan reported that a third child was seriously ill and requested a transfer, which he received to Inishowen East. Sadly, the couple lost another five children. The causes of the deaths of the seven children are unknown.

My thoughts also drifted to keepers who had died on the Skelligs, such as Michael Wishart, who is believed to have fallen to his death in the 1800s while cutting grass for his cow, and Séamus Rohu, who went missing in August 1956. His body was never found.

One summer's day, a 30-foot boat sailed in to Skellig Michael from Ballinskelligs with visitors on board, including two Americans. The other keepers and I greeted the group at the landing. Later, when I dived into the water to swim, one of the Americans joined me. As I watched him standing at the corner of the landing, preparing to dive, I realised he was the most perfect specimen of man I had ever seen. He was more than six feet in height, in his early twenties, strong, with a tightly toned body, like that of an athlete. On the day, there were at least 130 visitors on the rock and each and every one of them stood in awe of this man, flabbergasted by his appearance. When he dived in, he moved beautifully and swiftly through the water, in over-arm strokes.

On the following day, he returned again with his fellow American. Another keeper on the rock, Pat Kennedy from Wexford, was fooling around with me on the landing and threw me into the water. I dived down deep, swam across the entire landing, surfaced at the far-off side and swam back again, surfacing only when I reached the other end. When the American swimmer decided to have a go, he only managed to get half-way across without surfacing. He told me he was used to swimming on the surface but had no underwater training. He was great fun and later suggested we should have a drink. When I told him that I was a teetotaller, he laughed, ruffled my hair and said, 'An Irish man who doesn't drink? I don't believe it!'

Shortly afterwards, as I was watching the 1972 Munich Olympic Games on television, I spotted him competing in swimming events. I argued with myself that it could not possibly be the same guy. His name was Mark Spitz and that year he walked away with seven gold medals! Later, a hotel in Waterville phoned the lighthouse to say that he had been staying there as a stop-over on his way to Munich, when he visited Skellig Michael. I had been swimming with Mark the Shark, as he was fondly known, and never knew it.

But Mark Spitz wasn't the only visitor to the rock who made a lasting impression on me. One balmy, sunny afternoon, a boat from Derrynane sailed to the landing with visitors on board. A beautiful, tanned girl, with thick, shoulder-length, dark hair, dressed in denim shorts and a bright top, stood on the bow holding a rope, ready to throw it to one of the keepers. I felt as if I was looking at a romantic scene from a film in the South Sea Islands and was instantly swept away by the loveliness of the girl, who was about my own age. Having helped the visitors ashore, I immediately struck up a conversation with her, while the others made their way up to the lighthouse. She introduced herself as Úna from Dublin. Even her name was music to my ears. We chatted about our lives and she seemed keen to hear about the day-to-day running of the lighthouse.

All too soon, the time came for her to leave. By then, the tide had ebbed and the boat had dropped below the level of the landing. As she clutched the rope, the boat slid down on a small wave and squeezed her fingers between the rope and the landing. Her fingers bled profusely and I asked the boatman to wait while I took her for some bandages to the keepers' house, which was about a mile from the landing. Of course, this suited me down to the ground as I wanted to spend more time with her and find out her contact details. As we headed off on our trek, another keeper decided to tag along. I felt like asking him, 'Do you not know that three is a crowd?' Despite his presence, I managed to get her address and I promised to visit her when I returned to the Baily. As the boat sailed away from the lighthouse, I waved from the landing and framed her pretty picture in my mind, full of the joys of love.

Soon after, when I was being transferred from the Skelligs on relief duty to Fastnet, I went down to the small helicopter pad, as I was being picked up by a helicopter on its way to Inishtearaght with other keepers on board, including my brother Edmund. As part of my training, I had been instructed to walk around the front of a helicopter when boarding, to stay within the pilot's view. The only vacant seat was behind the pilot, which meant I should cross over to the far-off side. Because of the position of the helicopter on the pad, there was practically no room for me to walk in front of the helicopter. So I opted to cross at the rear instead.

The rotors spun constantly, as this was vital for a quick take-off if a problem arose. As I was making my way around the back, I suddenly stopped. My face was about an inch from the tail rotor. If I had taken another half step forward, I would have been sliced to bits. When I realised my predicament, I froze. Then, I went back and squeezed my way through in front of the helicopter and over to the pilot's side. I didn't breathe a word to anyone, as I didn't want anyone to know how close I had come to a major accident.

On a second term of duty on Inishtearaght, I decided to go diving for cray fish. Although the sea seemed beautiful and calm, there was a good rise and fall at the landing. Before I jumped in, I tied a rope to a stanchion, to help me escape if I failed to get out by myself.

I combed the water for the cray fish but caught nothing. I tried to swim ashore, but failed, as the sea was too rough and the huge surge of water kept pushing me back out. After many attempts at trying to get aground, I decided to wait until a massive wave came. Then, as it rolled near me, I grabbed hold of the rope and pulled myself towards the landing. As the wave subsided, it dragged me back out, but I was closer to the landing than previously and able to make it ashore before the next wave gushed forward.

On my return to the Baily, I dropped in to Úna's home in Dublin one Sunday evening, having phoned beforehand. My heart sank when she told me she was preparing to fly to Africa as a volunteer. She encouraged me to write to her about my life on the lighthouses, saying that what might seem ordinary to me would be of great interest to her. I've never forgotten her words, so much so that, when I give lectures on lighthouses, I always tell people that they should write their own story, as no two lives are the same. Although we exchanged many letters, we never met again. We were like ships passing in the night. On her return from Africa, she married and settled in Derrynane, the seaside village from which she had sailed to the Skelligs on the day we first met.

Time moved on and I was posted to Roancarrig lighthouse near Castletownbere in west Cork, the rock station where Daddy was working when I was born. During my time at Roancarrig, the Suez Canal blockage featured highly in the news. The blockage occurred after the 1967 Arab-Israeli war, when the canal was closed by an Egyptian blockade until 5 June 1975. Whiddy Island – which stood as the entrance to western Europe and had once facilitated an entire British fleet while anchored in Bantry Bay, the largest and deepest harbour in Ireland, in the pre-independent era – was selected as an oil depot for storing oil. I saw mammoth oil tankers, among them Universe Ireland, sail into Bantry Bay and off-load their oil onto Whiddy Island for storage. As these massive tankers came in, they stopped their engines about 20 miles off Fastnet, as the weight on these ships was heavy enough to bring them close to Bantry Bay, where they would be taken by tugs and hauled into the harbour. At night, the bay looked like a city, because of the mass of lights from the anchored ships. The oil was later shipped throughout Europe by smaller tankers.

On Roancarrig, we were responsible for logging the times of arrival and departures of all tankers on the southern side of Bantry Bay. As a further aid to navigation, a lighthouse was built on Sheep's Head especially for these gigantic tankers. It made a massive profit from their passing.

After twelve months with Irish Lights, I handed up my log book, which was signed by every principal keeper with whom I had worked. It showed my duties, all that I had learned on each lighthouse and my state of proficiency. Moving to the next level of the qualification process was subject to a favourable progress report, so I had wisely omitted all my adventurous antics and escapades from my records, as I knew they would reflect badly on me and make my superiors think twice about appointing me. Also, I sat an in-house exam, in which I was tested on Morse code, international code, semaphore, signals, radio telephony, first aid, derricks, landing stores and oils by boat and helicopter, watch keeping, ropes, burners, lights, lenses and engine maintenance.

Thankfully, I passed the test, which meant that I was no longer on probation and that I was now a supernumerary assistant keeper, or SAK as we were called. During this period, I would continue to be based at the Baily and be available for relief duty, which usually came about because of compassionate or sick leave. I was presented with my uniform for the very first time, which was made by Cleary's in Dublin. I was expected to wear the uniform when travelling to and from lighthouses, as well as during times of inspection by the commissioners.

As an SAK, I was required to serve another three years before automatically qualifying as an assistant keeper. During that time, I served at many stations all around the Irish coast, including some of the lighthouses in which I had worked before, as well as: Dún Laoghaire East Pier, Roche's Point, Power Head, Tuskar Rock, Hook Point, Ballycotton Island, Eeragh, Eagle Island, Blackrock Mayo, Fanad Head, Rockabill, the Old Head of Kinsale and Mizen Head.

On rock stations in particular, I found that time slowed down, so much so that I would lose all sense of the day of the week or the hour, as there was no rush on me to go anywhere or do anything. Coming ashore was strange, especially after several weeks on duty, as it meant having to instantly switch to a faster pace of life. In summertime, particularly in the month of June, I'd look in wonder at how high the grass on the sides of the road had grown while I was away. Whenever I went directly home or to the Baily from a rock station, I found it hard to cope with the constant noise and chatter, which was in stark contrast to the peace and tranquillity of the rock. But, after a couple of days, I'd be as loud as the rest of them. Then, when I'd return to a rock station, I'd find it just as hard to adjust to the quietness and to the fact that I was stranded. Due to the isolation of the rock stations, many of the SAKs preferred serving on the mainland lighthouses.

In 1972, while serving as an SAK on Mizen Head, several army trucks arrived to confiscate our fog signal explosives, as a decision had been taken to end the use of explosive signals on all light-houses around the Irish coast and to install electric fog signals in certain stations. We were witnessing and participating in the end of an era.

The other keepers and I opened up the two magazine stores. One of the stores housed electric detonators, all of which were stored in wooden boxes. We carried the boxes up to the top of the station and placed them in the waiting trucks. Then, we gathered the boxes of tonite charges from the other magazine hut. When the trucks pulled away with all our explosives, we were left without any fog signal.

Afterwards, a notice was issued to mariners stating that the use of explosive fog signals had ceased. The mariners never requested to have these signals restored, thereby suggesting that they were no longer required. Also, it appeared that mariners had stopped keeping an outside watch and operated from inside the wheel-house instead. However, an electric fog horn, with a high pitch, piercing sound, was later installed at certain lighthouses. Some stations that used compressed air to operate sirens and diaphone signals were also fitted with electric emitters, called Nautophones.

One Sunday morning, while my brother Edmund was on watch at the Baily, he spotted a small, empty, plywood boat drifting across Dublin Bay. The punt glided in under the cliffs, close to the gates of the Baily. Edmund immediately contacted the gardaí in Howth, as he felt they should be told. When the gardaí arrived, some wreckage was afloat out past the Baily. Mistakenly, the gardaí and Edmund assumed that this was the remains of the punt Edmund had told them about.

As it happened, I was also at the Baily on the same day. Later that evening when Edmund and I climbed down the cliffs, what should we find only the punt he had spotted that morning, sitting on the rocks, with a big hole driven through it, but still all in one piece. We studied the rocks and eventually figured out a way of pulling the boat up the huge, steep cliff.

At 5.00 a.m. on the following Tuesday, we climbed down the cliff with our gear, all set up to haul up the boat. We roped the punt tightly and began to lug it up the rocks. Half-way up the cliff, Edmund slid in under the boat and hoisted the front section on his shoulders. I lifted the stern and inch by inch we heaved the punt up the rocks. On the cliff top, we landed it onto the roof rack of the car and headed for Cork.

By the time we got home to Galley Head, we'd made great plans for the boat and intended fitting it with an outboard motor. But lo and behold, later in the week, as we were watching *Garda Patrol* one night, our prized punt appeared, with a plea from its owner for its return.

On the next day, Edmund popped in to the garda station in Rosscarbery and explained what had happened. We then contacted the owner and returned the boat to him in Dún Laoghaire. Although we told him the truth, he stared at us in disbelief, as he just couldn't get his head around the fact that his little punt had ended up in west Cork.

When my term as an SAK ended and I was appointed as an assistant keeper. I waited with bated breath to hear the name of the lighthouse to which I would be posted, full of expectation that a new and challenging adventure lay ahead. But, I was also conscious of the responsibility and seriousness of my new status, as I knew only too well the dangers and ruthlessness of the sea.

5

Bull Rock

When I was told that I was being posted as an assistant keeper to Bull Rock, off the extreme south-west coast of Ireland, I was thrilled to bits to be heading for the seas around the Beara Peninsula, which boasted three other rocks: The Cow, The Calf and The Heifer. I had a close family connection with the Bull, as my uncle Amby had served there many years before. Famous for the natural tunnel that runs through the end of the lighthouse, Bull Rock was built in 1888 near the mouth of Kenmare River, more than five miles from the mainland, and towers 300 feet above sea level. Although desolate in appearance, it attracts a huge variety of birds.

Having met the other keepers, I went off on my own and climbed down the two hundred steps, or more, leading to the main boat landing. As I stood at the water's edge and looked back up at the lighthouse, perched on a cut-out ledge and gazing calmly over the swelling Atlantic, I thought of the men who had built it. I marvelled at the craftsmanship and human effort involved in quarrying the local stone, cutting out the rock on such a hazardous location and hauling heavy building materials to the site, often in severe weather conditions. To the lightkeepers, civil engineers and tradesmen who followed, they left a legacy of high standards.

On the Bull, as on every lighthouse, attending the light, watch keeping and recording were central to the duties of a lightkeeper. In all, we were responsible for keeping over twenty records, including fog and engine logs, as well as records on every task undertaken, passing ships and unusual incidents. We entered most of our records on an hourly or a daily basis. As the station stored vast amounts of coal and oil, much time was also spent on unloading and hoisting supplies, cleaning engines of oil spills and topping up fuel storage tanks, as well as water tanks. At that time, the station had not yet been electrified and the winding weight lamp – which was an old system for rotating the lens – was still in use.

In evening time when the sun set, one of the keepers went inside the centre of the lantern and lit the light. He placed a lighted tray of methylated spirit under the retort to heat it. When the retort heated, the paraffin oil vaporized inside. Then, he opened the oil valve to allow oil to flow into the retort under pressure. Once the vaporized gas found its way into the mantles, the light was lighting.

When the keeper came out from inside the lantern, he went to the kitchen and moved in and out from there, keeping an eye on the station, particularly on the light, and looking out to sea to check if any ship was in difficulty. Then every 30 minutes, he returned to the lantern to wind up the weight.

At 10.00 p.m., the keeper signed off by taking a weather recording from the barometer, which hung on the kitchen wall, and logging it into the weather journal. Also, he took temperature readings and noted the state of the sea readings, as well as cloud cover, which was always entered as either blue sky, partly clouded or clouded. Then, he informed the oncoming keeper of the time at which the light should be wound again.

The 10.00 p.m. keeper continued the routine of watch keeping, winding the light every thirty minutes, pumping up air pressure and recording. His hourly weather report, which he entered into the fog signal journal, included the strength of the wind and visibility. In between watches, he usually chatted to the other two keepers, looked at television or played cards. His watch ended at

2.00 a.m., when he handed over to the next keeper, who repeated the duties until he signed off at 6.00 a.m. Then, the first keeper went back on duty again.

He extinguished the light by switching off the oil supply going into the light. The time for doing so varied, depending on sun light. He stopped the lens rotating by applying a brake to the governor of the machine and this halted the weight from descending down through the lighthouse. Then, he pulled the curtains to block the sun from shining back in through the lens and wound up the weight, ready for the keeper responsible for lighting up. Manually, he pumped 60 pounds of air pressure into an air receiver. He tidied and cleaned the kitchen, swept or mopped the floors and stairs, and ensured that all glazed surfaces were sparkling. After breakfast, he signed off, leaving everything in tip-top condition.

Usually around midday, all three keepers began preparing individual dinners and popped them into the gas cooker. Then, we started maintenance work on some of the equipment, although only one of us was officially on duty. We might change the oil in the engines or take the fog siren apart if there was a problem and replace parts. If maintenance personnel needed our assistance, we helped them.

After lunch, the keeper who had been on the 6.00 a.m. watch usually took a nap in his bunk for a few hours, to make up for lost sleep, while the other two keepers washed up. Sometimes, the keeper who went on duty at 2.00 a.m. took a rest later in the day, as it was vital to be fully alert while on duty.

If a relief keeper was due on the rock, the changeover usually took place every second Wednesday. That day was a good choice, as it broke up the week for the keepers coming on the rock or going ashore. On the week that a relief keeper was due, we spent Monday and Tuesday cleaning the station from top to bottom and polishing the brass and lens until they gleamed. We never left a speck of dust in our trail. When a relief keeper failed to make it to the rock on the expected day, usually due to bad weather or illness, it meant huge disappointment for the keeper waiting to go ashore, as well as for his family. Sometimes, due to severe weather, relief might be delayed for weeks. Once, in my father's time, the relief of assistant keeper Jim Dillon on Blackrock Mayo, who was supposed to be marrying on his first day ashore, was delayed by fifteen days due to storms. Reporters and cameramen got wind of the drama and laid in wait for Jim on Blacksod. When he eventually got to the church of Bighamstown, they were there before him. They attended the wedding breakfast, photographed the couple's departure from Ballina and greeted them at the railway station in Dublin when they arrived for their honeymoon.

Only months after I set foot on the Bull, plans were drawn up for its electrification. An electrician and apprentice arrived to prepare the station for the switch. They stayed for months, usually working four weeks at a time and then taking a liberty period. They re-wired the entire lighthouse and installed three generators in the engine room. The old clockwork motor was then dismantled and removed from the lighthouse, and a new electric motor was installed to turn the lens. We no longer had to light the light in the traditional way, as it now lit up with the flick of a switch. To the lightkeepers of my day, that was indeed a huge technological development.

By and large, working on the Bull meant repeating the same duties over and over again, day in and day out, meticulously. I quickly became familiar with the routine. But living on the rock was not as straightforward, especially as one of my fellow keepers was temperamental.

On my first day on the Bull, the principal keeper Paddy Brennan advised me to avoid getting into a row with fellow keepers. Even if we didn't see eye to eye, he said it was best to let any wrangling fly over my head. I took his advice on board and it stood to me well, although at times I found it hard to avoid a squabble, especially as the other assistant was fairly fiery.

One night, we had a tiff about a televised, cross-channel soccer match. I knew I was right and defended my view. But he continued to challenge me. After a few minutes, it became blatantly obvious that a blazing row was about to erupt. Paddy happened to wander in, sensed a storm was brewing and gave me the wink. So I made a wisecrack, swiftly changed the topic in a jovial kind of way and strolled out for a breath of fresh air. By the time I came back, it had all blown over.

Having a game of cards often ended in a heated spat, especially if the other assistant keeper thought he was being cheated, even though we gambled for only a few pence a game. But I soon learned to recognise the signs of a looming row and spotted he was on the boil if he pursed his lips, as that signalled an attack.

Once, I told him that I'd seen the sun shine on Mine Head at 7.10 a.m. on a November morning, which was true. I knew it would get the wind up him and waited to see his reaction. He nearly had a seizure and insisted that I had to be wrong. He grew so frantic that I quickly gave in and agreed that I must have been mistaken.

But Paddy was right, because it was pointless rowing with fellow keepers, especially as we had to work and live together on the rock, day in and day out, for a month at a time. I read once that any argument between two people is futile, as the outcome is always irrelevant, unless a third person is present who knows the solution. The more I thought about it, the more I realised it was true.

One of the first traits that struck me about Bull Rock was that part of the rock bellowed, as the waves compressed air into a certain crevice in the rock. On release, it let out a huge, bellowing, haunting sound. During one ferocious storm in winter, gigantic, crashing waves ripped off rock and wedged it into the blow hole, putting an end to its bellowing forever.

Down near the landing, a small pool filled at high tide, making it ideal for swimming. Although it was deep, it was safe. Then, another vicious storm tore rocks from the side of the cliff and blocked up the pond permanently.

One day as Paddy Brennan and I were being flown to the Bull by helicopter, the pilot approached the rock from the east to make a landing. The wind blew from the west, at about force 7, not extremely strong. As the wind struck the western face of the cliff, most of the wind rose, as more wind pushed in behind it. Right at the top, on the helicopter pad, it felt like a gale, with wind rising vertically and being funnelled high into the sky. As the helicopter neared the landing pad, the tips of its rotors were sticking out and caught this updraft of air from the platform, making it impossible for the pilot to land safely. Inside the helicopter, we were riddled with massive vibrations. The pilot decided to abort the landing, so he moved the helicopter forward and flew down the side of the cliff, into the surging wind. When we reached the bottom, he corrected the helicopter and flew out over the water. Then, he returned to make a second attempt at landing. I felt sorry for Paddy, who was sitting in front, as his nerves were certainly tested, even though he looked calm. On the second attempt, the pilot had the same problem and failed to land. On the third attempt, he made up his mind to land, even though he opted for the same approach. At about five feet from the pad, he pressed down the lever. Having lost the pitch in the main rotor, the helicopter did not fall directly onto the pad but floated like a leaf from side to side. When it landed, the right-hand skid barely caught the landing pad. Later that day, another pilot with more experience landed without any difficulty. Instead of approaching the pad from the side, he flew down directly from above.

The sea around the Bull was always unpredictable. One morning, a wave rose to a height of about 180 feet, gushed over the rock, filled the two gasometers in the back yard and then quietly slipped away down the north side of the rock without causing any damage.

A gannet colony nested on the western side of Bull Rock, which is a very sheer rock, about 200 feet high, with small ledges, ideal for gannets to build their nests. Gannets can only take off from the face of a cliff or from the sea. When they dive into the ocean, they do so from great heights and with tremendous speed. If they land in a field or roadway, they fail to become airborne.

One evening after supper, as I climbed down to the landing to fish, I spotted a gannet tangled in netting, high up the rock, with some seagulls perched nearby, waiting to make a meal of him. I caught the gannet and tried to free him from the netting. He was a lump of a bird, with tiny, beady eyes and a long, sharp, point-ed beak, most beautiful and unusual. With one hand, I clutched his beak and clasped it tight, unaware that gannets can breathe only through their mouths, as their noses are actually inside their mouths. I struggled to free him from the mesh. But, every few minutes, he'd break away from my clutch and bite my hand with his razor-sharp beak. Then, I'd grab him again and hold his beak tight, until he bit me one more time. Finally, I managed to free him and watched him flutter happily away, having denied the seagulls their expected food. As my hand was pumping blood, I headed back up to the kitchen for some bandages.

The deep waters around Bull Rock were rich in cray fish. To catch these big, shell fish, it was necessary to swim 40 feet below the surface. Every day, I jumped off the cliff and snorkel-dived to hunt for them. Usually, I caught four or five. In the summer months, they were so plentiful that we ate like kings. Bream and pollock were also bountiful.

Often, I put on my diving suit to insulate me from the cold and swam out far away from the rock, equipped with a fishing line and a plastic, market basket. Then, I lowered the fishing line down into the water and jigged for pollock. Looking down from the surface, I could see the fish trying to swim away in every direction, to make a swift escape. I'd haul them up with all my might, as they were huge in size, and throw them into my basket. Looking up at Bull Rock, with only my head above the water, it looked massive, powerful, almost threatening. Its enormity overwhelmed me and filled me with the same sense of awe I had felt as a child when I gazed up at the dark pier at Ballycotton, as I sailed away with Daddy to spend a week with him on the rock. The other keepers were always delighted when I returned with the pollock. Sometimes, the catch was so big that I froze some of the fish and took some home to my parents, as the pollock at the Galley was always much smaller.

At night on the Bull, before taking a lie-down around 11.00 p.m., ahead of the 2.00 a.m. watch, I'd lay the table for a cup of tea, grab my fishing rod from the back porch and nip down to the landing. With just one throw of the line, I'd catch a pollock. Then, I'd dash back up to the kitchen, toss the fish around in the frying pan and have it cooked in only a matter of minutes.

Being an assistant keeper on Bull Rock gave me the luxury of having my own bedroom, which meant I had my own private space and could leave my belongings behind when I left the rock on my time off. Because of having my own room, I arrived on the Bull well equipped for a long stay and quickly turned my bedroom into a workshop. It proved a wise decision, especially as a good night's sleep was out of the question, because the siren fog signal at the Bull, with its triple cast-iron trumpets, was one of the loudest signals and every time it sounded, the lighthouse vibrated.

Among the heap of tools I brought along was a miniature vice. When I needed to cut a piece of timber, I attached the vice to the table, fitted in the timber, gripped it tightly with the vice and then shaved off the wood to the required size. I also brought along some lead, from which I made fishing sprats, with two hooks sticking out at the ends. And I made ornamental weapons, mostly steel knives with brass handles. First, I softened an old file with a blow lamp, until it became pliable enough to shape it with another file. Then, I riveted together sections of flat brass with brass rivets, to make a brass handle. After I joined the handle to the knife, I polished and shined the brass and steel until they sparkled.

One of the prized possessions I stored in my bedroom was an old, broken, tea clipper, square-rigged model ship, built by my fraternal grandfather in the late 1800s, handed down to my father and kept in a box at home for years. A tea clipper was a swift sailing ship, with at least three masts and a square rig. The boom years of the tea clipper ships started in 1843, due to the demand for a more rapid delivery of tea from China. I decided to reconstruct the model ship. But first, I had to find out everything about it. All through history, styles of ships changed, as there was always a quest for speed, a need to cut time, to get to a destination quicker. I scoured through an ancient, nautical almanac for names of shipbuilding companies in England. Many of the firms listed were no longer in business. Some may have been bombed during the Second World War. I requested plans and rigging diagrams for sailing ships of the Tall Ships period, which ran from the 1800s to the late 1920s, when steam ships came into being, and also included barques and brigs. My search led me to a nautical publishing company in Scotland, named Brown Son and Ferguson Limited, and I bought plans from them for many sailing ships. Once, during a month off, I sailed by ferry on the Innisfallen and then drove to visit the *Cutty Sark*, which was preserved in dry dock at Greenwich, London and is the world's last tea clipper ship. I spent a full evening examining the *Cutty Sark*, checking its rigging and every detail of construction. I scoured through all the information posted about the ship in display cases, which contained data on how it was built and how it worked. I tried to visualise myself as one of the mariners who sailed on the *Cutty Sark*, to get a sense of how they must have felt and how they went about their work.

Once I was satisfied that I had gathered as much information as possible, I set about reconstructing my grandfather's model ship. During bleak winter nights, I spent many off-duty hours in my bedroom, totally engrossed in rebuilding the ship, a task that would take me two years to complete. If I couldn't sleep at night, I'd gaze at the ship, which I always kept on the table beside me, and try to figure out how I would craft the next piece. Sometimes, I imagined myself on the ship, climbing its rigging to trim its sails or sailing in stormy seas to China, battling to survive the wrath of the sea.

To begin the reconstruction, I made all the masts from ordinary, white deal timber. I crafted the sails from parchment and attached them to spars. To create the rigging, I used the exact same method my father had used to make hemp for cobbling shoes. I paid great attention to detail, right down to the tiniest feature, as I was determined to make an exact replica. I even carved out little timber lifeboats to place on the ship's deck and a figurehead, just like I had seen in the *Cutty Sark*.

For its figurehead, the *Cutty Sark* used a statue of a witch. According to legend, one evening a farmer was riding home on horseback when he spotted some nude maidens dancing around a fire on an island in a river. After crossing the bridge to the island, he realised they were witches and turned his horse around to flee for his life. One of the maidens raced after him. As she drew near, she stretched out her hand and grabbed the horse's tail, which came away in her hand. Over her shoulder, she wore a short piece of material, known as a cutty sark, and so evolved the name and figurehead of the *Cutty Sark*. When the *Cutty Sark* sailed into a port, the sailors always climbed out onto the bow of the ship and placed a piece of rope in the hand of the figurehead, as a symbol of the horse's tail.

With my own figurehead firmly in place and all the rebuilding finished, I named the model ship *Analiza*, in memory of my grandmother, and I handed back the ship to my father. In both Ireland and England, it's traditional to give a ship a feminine name, whereas in Germany the opposite is true.

First Communion – Edmund and Gerald with Dominic O'Connor

Twins Edmund and Gerald, 1952

Butler family in 1967

Granddad Fitzgerald

Larry Butler

*Mam and Dad – From a Day in the
Life of Ireland*

Mam in front of Galley Head Lighthouse

Granuaile, CIL ship

Galley Head

Fastnet Rock

Mine Head

Fastnet commemoration

The monument plaque reads:

Paul Baldwin
Robin Bowyer
Sub-Lt Russell Brown
David Crisp
Peter Dorey
Peter Everson
Frank Ferris
William Le Fevre
John Puxley
Robert Robie
David Sheahan
Sub-Lt Charles Steavenson
Roger Watts
Gerrit-Jan Williahey
Gerald Winks

Galley Head at night

Old Head

Gerald at Fastnet

Gerald with his model ship

Denis Downey and Gerald at Mizen Head Visitors Centre

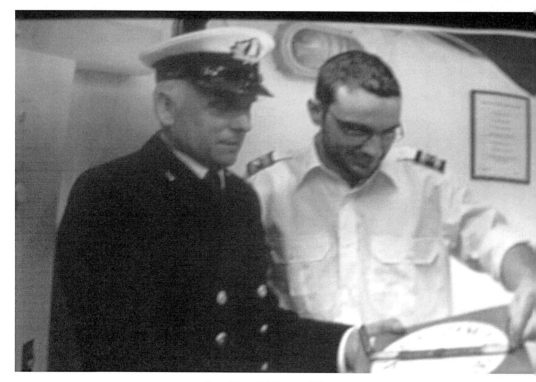

Gerald and his son Aidan

Gerald at Galley

Many superstitions exist about women and shipping, perhaps the most widely known superstition being that a woman on board brings bad luck and angers the seas, as she serves only as a distraction to the crew. Such bad luck can be counteracted only by having a naked woman on board. Because of this superstition, many ships have bare breasted women as their figureheads. Also, a redhead on the harbour as a ship sets sail is considered to be a sign of bad luck for the ship, but such bad luck can be reversed if a crew member speaks to the redhead first, rather than allow her initiate a conversation. Superstitions exist too among fishermen and some refrain from learning to swim to avoid challenging the spirits of the sea.

As well as the broken model ship, I also brought an inflatable rubber dingy to the rock, even though lightkeepers were forbidden to have a boat there, as being in a boat meant that you were no longer attached to the lighthouse. One evening, as the other assistant keeper and I were out in the dingy, we spotted a school of whales speeding towards us. These huge creatures encircled us from a distance of three yards, rose up from the depths, smashed through the surface and dived underneath again. We were fascinated to see them at close range and to glimpse the swiftness at which they travelled. Luckily for us, they were not killer whales.

After being out in the dinghy one morning, I got a phone call from the Lucey family, whom I had met previously. They ran a business in Limerick and at the time were staying at their holiday home in Derrynane. They were sailing to the Bull by yacht, with some guests on board. Landing conditions on the day were ideal. At the time, Tom Tweedy, or Tucks as he was known to all, was the acting principal keeper and the two of us climbed down to the landing to greet the group. Straight away, I started up a casual conversation with one of the party, who seemed a gentle, pleasant man, with a soft-spoken voice. I spotted some of the others smiling at me. They knew by my manner that I had no idea that I was talking to someone very important – so important that he was accompanied by bodyguards. The man with whom I was chatting was actually President Cearbhall Ó Dálaigh, the fifth president of Ireland. His wife was also part of the group. Both of them were enthralled by the rock and keen to see the big, arch tunnel that ran through its centre at sea level. Bean Uí Dálaigh, who was very much into folklore, told us that legend had it that souls passed through this channel on their way to hell. Later, in years to come, when I started giving lectures about lighthouses, I would recall her tale and add to it by saying that the lightkeepers on the Bull shook hands with the souls as they passed through the arch. In Celtic mythology, Bull Rock, or Teach Donn as it was known, was the underworld residence of the spirits of the dead, while early Irish Christians associated it with purgatory.

The arch contained a huge cave, about 30 feet high. Massive waves pumped through it, then gushed out to the east at the other side. Sometimes, I fished by lowering my rod from the top of the hoist house, about 120 feet above sea level and right over the arch. I dropped my sprat into the water and started jigging. As the water flowed speedily through the arch, my sprat kept getting swept away from the hollow. When I let it settle near the bottom at a long distance out, I caught several big pollock.

One morning, a kittiwake became entangled in my gut line, just as I was lowering it over the arch. As I hauled up the line to free the small seagull, he threw up a bellyful of tiny fish. The amount of food he had swallowed surprised me and opened my eyes to the fact that the thousands of birds on the Bull at the time must all have had their bellies just as full.

In spring, these birds landed on the cliff and built their nests on the ledges. When I walked over to the landing area, the racket and clatter of those birds reminded me that the cliff was their territory and that they lived there together, busily rearing their young and teaching them to fly. I watched them as they fluttered excitedly through the air with their friends and visited each others nests.

Paddy Brennan had watched these birds over the years and knew that each year, without fail, on the 23 August, they disappeared. When they left, it was the loneliest feeling ever, as emptiness and silence fell on the cliff, robbing it of its core. Even though the weather may still have been fine and the evenings still bright, their departure marked the onset of winter.

One winter, in thick fog, a few hundred jackdaws landed on the Bull. It seemed they were lost. They stayed there for about ten days, waiting for the fog to clear. Sadly, by the time visibility was good enough for them to return to the mainland, they were too weak to take flight, as they were starving. When some of them died, others of their flock ate their remains. One evening, a strong wind from the west blew onto the face of the cliff. Jackdaws fly in the shelter of the wind and when the wind rose up, one of them flew out into the updraft and was catapulted about 70 feet into the air. This never happened to sea gulls or any natural birds in the area. Within a week, all of the jackdaws had died from hunger. Perhaps, it was nature's way of culling.

In the spring, the other two keepers and I painted all the outside of the lighthouse and surrounding walls white, as it was important for mariners to be able to spot the lighthouse from afar. Also, we needed to prevent the onset of rust. We cleaned and polished everything in sight, although we always kept the lighthouse in tip-top condition, regardless of the time of year. The light at Bull Rock was a treble, fifty burner, with a huge lens that weighed about eight tons. Cleaning the light was difficult, as it had to be done by standing on a vertical ladder at a height of 20 feet.

During the summer, I returned to Galley Head to relieve my father while he took his holidays, a tradition I continued every other year. By then, I had my own little fishing boat and dived often. I'd sail out a good distance from the Galley, tie a rope onto the stern of the boat, hold the other end, dive right down to the bottom and explore the ocean floor, as the boat moved along with the current. I came across boulders there the size of a house. I'd swim up the side of them, cross over on top and swim down the other side. But I never spotted anything of interest, other than marine life. Other times, I went cray fishing with our neighbour Pat Joe Harrington and sold the catch to Donal Sheehy, a buyer from Baltimore.

In the month of June or July, the inspector and marine super-intendent, along with the engineer-in-chief, came with the commissioners of Irish Lights to inspect the Bull, as part of their tour of lighthouses around the coast. One year, they'd begin the trip by sailing south from Dublin. The next year, they'd head north first. They were accompanied by a large crew and always arrived on the *Granuaile* – a tender ship owned by Irish Lights and used to deliver stores and service aids to navigation at sea. Word would spread like wildfire all around the coast that they had left the Baily and were on their way. Everything went into overdrive then and not a minute was wasted, as we wanted the lighthouse gleaming from top to bottom, with not a speck of dust in sight. With all the preparation complete and all glazing sparking like the sun, we un-rolled the Irish Lights' flag and hoisted it on top of the mast, ready to welcome the visiting party. Once we spotted their approach, the other two keepers and I made our way to the boat landing to greet them, dressed in our uniform. They were also dressed in uniform, but it differed to ours, as the buttons on their blazers were black, not brass, and their slacks were grey, while ours were navy.

Over a few hours, the inspection party checked every single item at the station. The inspection entailed making sure that all the equipment was in perfect working order and that the buildings at the station were in ship-shape condition. They examined our annu-al supply of medicines, which contained morphine. The drug was stored only on rock stations, as opposed to land stations, and had to be administered under the advice of a doctor. Also, they checked if the existing equipment and living accommodation at the station were adequate. They made sure that all the jobs listed in the previous year were completed and they listed all the tasks to be completed prior to the next inspection. They went about their work in a pleasant, friendly manner, with the attitude that they were there to help us, rather than find fault with us. If we needed a replacement or new items for the lighthouse, they noted it in their pocket books. That way of ordering essentials proved faster than any bureaucratic procedure, so we always made sure to list all our needs well in advance of their arrival, as this was our fast track to getting what we wanted. Once they left, we got word to the next station that they were on their way, took down the flag and rolled it up for storage. Then, we got on with enjoying the rest of the summer.

Looking back, the summers seemed beautiful then. We lived in our togs and during our leisure time basked under the sun on an old roof, at the top of the cliff. Some people went to the tropics to sunbathe. We were paid to do it on the Bull.

In the evenings, when we were off duty, we lounged on the cliff top on the western side, near the helicopter pad, and watched the gannets fluttering over and back to their nests, stealing building material from each other, or fighting with neighbouring birds.

One evening in late autumn, I saw a huge stream of birds flying down to the mouth of Kenmare River. They were met by a big flock of other birds of the same species and they all flew south together to migrate. It was breath-taking to see the length of their flock.

After more than four years on the Bull, I decided it was time to move on myself. I felt like a change. As it happened, an assistant keeper on the Fastnet also wanted to move. We both applied for a transfer and were granted permission to swap. And so, I returned to the forbidding Fastnet Rock, on which I had already served during my first two years with Irish Lights. My time there would prove to be one of the most challenging and memorable of my career.

6

Fastnet Rock

Whenever I served on Fastnet, I experienced danger. My spell there beginning in 1975 was no exception.

On my return to Fastnet, as I stepped out of the helicopter and onto the landing pad, the strength of the wind nearly blew me off the rock. Being only over nine stone in weight, I feared that a stronger wind might knock me off some day. So I took the decision to erect a removable safety rail on the helicopter platform that very day, by inserting steel poles into sockets on the edge of the pad and running a rope through the eyelets on top. And I heeded the principal keeper when he warned me to keep looking over my shoulder while walking on the helicopter platform, as a wave could gush high over the rock at any time and I would need to brace myself for the onslaught.

In contrast to the Bull, where I'd had my own bedroom, I found little privacy on Fastnet, as I had to share a bedroom with the other keepers. All three beds were strapped to the wall and had drawers fitted underneath. As I had brought few clothes to the rock, I stored my tools and equipment there instead. At night, if my sleep went astray on me or if I became restless, I'd switch on my small, four-inch radio and television set and tune into Radio Luxembourg or some other foreign station. I was spoiled for choice, because the reception on Fastnet was excellent and I could pick up many overseas channels. If the night was bright, I often got up and went outside, usually to dream up some escapade for my leisure time the next day.

On Fastnet, a rope hung permanently from the balcony to winch up all in-coming provisions. I climbed down that rope many times, just for the fun of it. One day, I decided to have a shot at scaling upwards instead. I had no bother, until I reached about 20 feet from the peak and the muscles in my fore-arm ceased. I just couldn't hold on any longer. I knew I shouldn't look down at the jagged rock and churning sea, about 90 feet below me, but I did. The possibility of a fall scared the hell out of me. But a sixth sense told me to wrap my leg around the rope for support. As I did so, I took my hands off the rope, because the pain in my fore-arm was too severe for me to clutch on any longer. As I fell back, with only my leg secured to the rope, I managed to hook the rope with my inner elbow, to hold me. I stayed in that position for a few minutes, until the muscles in my fore-arm unlocked. Rather than continue climbing up, I opted to go down, as I felt that every foot down was one foot less to fall. As I slid down the rope, my trousers lifted up to my knee. By the time I reached the bottom of the rock, the friction of the rope had torn all the skin off my leg. I was due on watch at 10.00 p.m. and sat motionless until the other lads went to their bunks. Then, I headed straight for the medicine chest, took some wooden splints we stored for breakages and tied them to my knee and ankle with stockings, so that nothing would touch my gashes. Luckily, it was the era of bell bottom trousers and I put on a pair of flared jeans to cover my wounds, as I knew I'd be in big trouble with the principal keeper if he found out what I had done.

In summertime, we swam often. One day, while I was swimming with the other two keepers, a fishing boat from Cape Clear stopped near us and entangled its propeller on a mooring rope. I offered to go underneath to check the damage and try to free the rope. As I ducked under the vessel, the coldness of the water hit me in a flash. So I swam to the surface and asked the lads on the boat for a knife, to speed things up. With the knife in my hand, I dived beneath again and started to cut the rope. The cold ran through me. The blood stopped flowing to my hands and the knife slipped back in my hand, which meant I was now clutching the blade. As well as cutting the rope, I was also slicing through my fingers. Eventually, I managed to free the boat. I swam to the surface, handed back the knife and swam towards the landing. When I reached it, I began to climb up the steps. By then, I was shivering violently. When I opened my hand to look at it, I could see all the sinews and veins, as well as everything inside my fingers, but no blood gushed out. Realising that I was on the verge of hypothermia, I raced up to the kitchen, switched on the electric cooker and stood there until I warmed up. Then, my fingers bled profusely.

At 5.00 a.m. one morning, while I was on watch, I wandered down to the landing. As the sea was so calm and beautiful, I couldn't resist jumping in. I had swam only a little away from the landing when I spotted two fins of a ten-foot shark swimming close by. It frightened the daylights out of me and I swam as fast as I could back to the landing. I never breathed a word to the principal keeper Reggie Sugrue, for fear of having my head bitten off.

On night duty, we always kept an eye on our generator sets. This meant going down through the inside of the lighthouse to the engine room to check the voltage and frequency of the generators, as well as the water circulation. Usually, we carried out this check once every twenty minutes. One night, I decided to do it in record time. Instead of walking down from the balcony, I slid down the rock on a rope and went into the lighthouse through a door at the bottom, as we always left the door open to circulate air. Then, I came up through the engine room. When I passed Reggie, he jumped and said, 'Where the hell did you spring from? I never saw you going down.' I tried to persuade him that I had spoken to him on the way down – a trick Edmund had successfully played before on another principal keeper. He looked very puzzled and followed me up to the kitchen. In only a matter of minutes, it clicked and he quickly gave me a piece of his mind. But we never fell out over it.

One night, shortly before Christmas, we knew that the weather was deteriorating rapidly and that the sea would soon whip high over the helicopter platform. After supper, Reggie and I went onto the helicopter pad to remove the stanchions and rail, as they would have been burst to bits by the might of the sea. As we tried to force our way back to the lighthouse through the wind, Reggie struggled on ahead of me. A big, sturdy man, he found it much easier than me to plod his way along. Being small and light, I could barely move. I clung tightly to the handrail that ran along the side of the rock and tried to pull myself forward. Outside that rail, another rail, made of steel cable, ran along the edge of the passage.

The wind swirled around the entrance door at the bottom of the lighthouse, and, in so doing, whisked up some extra strength. By the time I neared the door, Reggie was already inside. To get to the door, I would have to let go of the rail and walk about six paces without support. Each time I tried it, the vicious wind blew me back sideways and thrashed me against the safety rail on the edge. Being in my twenties and craving adventure, I got a great kick out of battling with the wind. I decided to take it on again, to have another shot at trying to get through the door. I tried and tried again to get inside, but each time the whirling wind pushed me sideways beyond the door. I knew I wouldn't get away with it forever. If I slipped under the rail, the wind would swiftly sweep me into the surging tide. I decided to give it a final lash. If I failed, I'd give up and spend the night in one of the stores. I let go of the handrail again and took a few paces forward. By then, Reggie had missed me. Just as I was being blown past the door, Reggie stuck his head out, in the direction of the wind. If he had looked the other way, the violent wind would have ripped off his glasses. He got the fright of his life when he saw me being swept towards him, with my feet barely touching the ground. He stretched out his left hand, grabbed me and shouted, 'Crisht you bastard get in that door!' And he hauled me in under his arm.

We locked up the waterproof, storm doors, which were fitted with about five different locking devices, mainly wheels and bolts. Then, we climbed up inside the lighthouse to make our way to the kitchen at the top of the tower, right under the lantern, at about 163 feet above sea level. When we got to the fourth flight, on which I had built a small work bench, I told Reggie I'd stay there for a few hours to work on the model ship I was making. He continued on for the kitchen.

I had been sitting at my bench for only ten minutes, when a huge wave soared over the rock. If we had been outside at that stage, we would have been washed away, because the strength and volume of the water was massive.

Around 9.00 p.m., I climbed up the stairway to the kitchen, as I wanted a cup of tea. From then on, every single wave that crashed onto the lighthouse swept high over the top. The tower swayed to and fro.

Then, about 11.00 p.m., as I was standing in the kitchen, a gigantic, powerful, deafening wave thrashed higher than any of the others and rocked the lighthouse like never before. I had to stretch out my leg to balance myself, as its vibrations were enormous. Sea water gushed up through every peephole, reminding us of our powerlessness, as nature took its course.

All through the night, the waves hammered violently and the lighthouse quivered, over and back, endlessly. I was due to start my watch duty at 6.00 a.m. and needed to get some sleep. I headed for the bedroom, but, instead of going to bed, I squeezed myself into the three-foot gap between the window pane and the outside bronze, storm shutter, which was water-tight, with small panes of storm glazing. By now, the sky overhead had cleared and the moon shone brightly, casting a shadow over Fastnet. The water was white and foamy. I opened the storm shutters and stuck out my head. I could see all the way out to Crookhaven and Rock Island, as well as east to Cape Clear.

When a wave approached the lighthouse, before it ever struck the tower, it rose up high and blotted out the moon. I closed the shutter and waited until the wave and its thunderous sound subsided. Then, I opened the shutter again and feasted my eyes on the collar of foam that swirled around the lighthouse, about three quarters of a mile in radius, imprisoning the tower. I never saw the sea so angry and stayed up all night, watching each wave as it pounded up over the lighthouse, totally submerging it, and then collapsing to make way for another onslaught.

About 9.00 a.m., the wind shifted in towards the north-west and blew with such force that it swiftly knocked down the sea. Later that morning, conditions were good enough for a helicopter to land on the rock.

One morning, having been on night watch, I woke at 11.00 a.m. as a massive wave smashed up over the top of the lighthouse and blotted out all light from the bedroom. Once the wave broke up and fell down, the room seemed to dazzle in whiteness. Then, another wave came and blacked out the light again. That sequence went on for hours.

But severe and stormy weather was common on Fastnet. Once, while I was on watch from 2.00 a.m. to 6.00 a.m., conditions became so violent that I tuned into the distress frequency on the radio, as I felt certain somebody at sea would be in trouble. Sure enough, around 4.00 a.m., a Greek ship named *Tina* broadcasted a May Day message in the Bay of Biscay, where the Irish national sail training ship, the *Asgard II*, sank in 2008. The *Tina* had taken a 30-degree list, or lean-over, due to winds of force 10 gusting on an enormous sea. An oil tanker on its way to Foynes responded to the May Day call and said it would be there in two hours. Brest Radio in France also answered the call and confirmed that the tanker was on its way. It acknowledged the ship's position and asked for more details about its location and situation. But, *Tina* never replied. Seemingly, the cargo on the ship shifted and, when the next wave struck, the vessel capsized, sinking the ship and its crew of fifteen. Not knowing this at the time, I kept listening to find out if the ship would be saved. For hours on end, Brest Radio kept calling *Tina*. It received no answer. There was no let-up in the weather and the sea continued to batter the lighthouse all through the night, gushing up the tower to a height of 160 feet, or more.

At 6.30 a.m. the tanker reached the area and began its search. It found no trace of *Tina*, no ship and no crew. As the morning progressed, the tanker picked up some bodies. After coming off my watch, I went to bed. When I rose again at 10.00 a.m., the search was continuing. The tanker requested permission from its owners to land the located bodies in Brest, saying that they were so badly mutilated that they would be decomposed by the time they reached Foynes.

During that day, the winds abated somewhat around Fastnet, but the sea kept battering around the door. We were unable to get out of the tower, due to the danger of being washed away, even if we only opened the door. Being confined in the tower was a regular occurrence. Once the sea calmed down, we were able to enjoy the freedom of getting out and about on top of the rock again.

Another time, a storm rolled in from the south-east. Being on the western side of the rock, the tower was sheltered. However, the sea broke up over the landing and helicopter pad, making it impossible for us to get out, as the door was under water. We had to stay indoors for three days, until the winds shifted and the sea fell.

When we headed out to check the damage, we found that the sea had burst in through the storm shutters on the windows of the stores under the helicopter platform. It floated every item kept there and smashed the inside of the stores. Bolts holding in place a heavy-grade steel, storm door, a quarter of an inch thick, were ripped out of the side of the wall. The door, which was larger than the opening, was pressed in through the opening, into the store room. We were amazed by the destructiveness of the storm, especially as the tower was sheltered by the rock. But the gale caused a hell of a lot of damage.

In finer weather, I used to swim off the landing at Fastnet and fish, mainly for pollock. But fishing gear lasted only for a short time, as the seaweed regularly entangled it, which meant we were often without fish when we wanted it.

One afternoon, as I was standing on the balcony, a little, timber dinghy landed at Fastnet and two young men got out. I invited them up to the kitchen for a cup of tea and a chat. Later, when the other assistant keeper, Donie Holland, and I went down to the landing with them, I asked if we could take the boat for a spin, just to circle the rock. They obliged and stayed on the rock as we set off in the dinghy.

We knew only too well that we were breaking the rules, as keepers on a rock station were not allowed leave it without the permission of the principal keeper. But we had no fears on that count, as Reggie had gone to bed ahead of his night watch and would not miss us. The boys could keep watch, we decided.

We paddled that dinghy a long distance away from the rock. We called to fishing boats and pleasure boats as we rowed along and gathered a good few pollock from them. Four hours later, we were still on the sea. We could see the two boys marching over and back on the pad, demented to be stuck on the rock, wondering if they would ever see their dinghy again. When we rowed back to the landing, we threw the fish up on the rock and thanked the lads profusely for the loan of the boat. They never said a word and took off as fast as they could. Reggie was still in his bunk and we had enough fish to last us a few days.

One morning, after starting a 6.00 a.m. watch, I got a bad pain in my stomach. It became so severe that I rang the doctor in Bantry and asked him to arrange to bring me ashore to Castletownbere. At the time, a new system had just been introduced whereby the local health authority took responsibility for bringing sick keepers ashore, instead of Irish Lights. But, when it came to the crunch, the health authority washed its hands of any such duty and I was left high and dry, stranded on Fastnet, doubled up in pain.

On the day, Irish Helicopters happened to be flying out to service the oil rigs off Kinsale. When the crew heard of my plight, they offered to pick me up. But for some reason or other, permission for them to do so was refused.

About 4.00 p.m. an Irish air corps helicopter was dispatched from Baldonnel to airlift me to hospital. As I stood on the helicopter pad, waiting for it to arrive, the pain became so intense that I ended up banging my head against the side of the old, iron lighthouse. Strangely enough, once the Alouette 3 helicopter came into view, the pain eased a little.

When I got out of the helicopter at Saint Finbarr's hospital in Cork, an ambulance was standing by. Although, I was now on the grounds of the hospital, I still had to be admitted by ambulance. As the helicopter flew away, the ambulance crew looked around in puzzlement for the patient and were amazed to find that I was the person to be admitted, as they didn't expect somebody dressed in uniform and I didn't look as if I was in pain.

By the time a doctor examined me in the accident and emergency room, the pain had disappeared and I was told a proper diagnosis would be possible only when I was in pain.

Some time later, while I was at home at Galley Head, one of the inspectors from Irish Lights dropped in. I told him that the system of airlifting ill keepers ashore was crazy and vowed that if I ever found myself in the same situation again, I'd put on my diving gear, jump into the water and stay there until I was picked up by a lifeboat. He just smiled at me and said, 'Now Gerry, I don't think it will ever come to that.'

On 8 January 1979, while I was at Galley Head during another period of leave, I noticed a thick, black, heavy plume of smoke rising up into the clouds and running inland, north-east. To my horror, I discovered that a French oil tanker named the *Betelgeuse* had exploded at 1.00 a.m. that morning, at the off-shore jetty oil terminal on Whiddy Island, while unloading a cargo of crude oil. The explosion and resulting inferno killed 50 people: 42 French nationals; seven Irish nationals and one United Kingdom national. Only 27 bodies were recovered. A failure in the ship's structure during the discharge operation was identified as the cause of the explosion. Sadly, a further fatality occurred during the salvage operation, when a Dutch diver lost his life. A single-point mooring buoy for loading and off-loading has since been installed at the terminal.

After the massive hull of the *Betelgeuse* was brought to the surface, it was sealed up and towed out beyond the Fastnet. As the other Fastnet keepers and I watched the hull being blown up and sunk, we shuddered to think of the scale of the tragedy. We were unaware then that another dreadful disaster was soon to strike, this time on the turbulent seas around the Fastnet.

7

Fastnet '79

The famous, Fastnet yachting competition first began in 1925 and runs every two years over a course of 608 nautical miles. The race starts at Cowes in the Isle of Wight in England, rounds the midway point at Fastnet Rock, returns to England through the south side of the Isles of Scilly and finishes at Plymouth.

When the 1979 Fastnet race began on Saturday 11 August, I was on duty as an assistant keeper on the Fastnet Rock lighthouse with the principal keeper, Reggie Sugrue, and a temporary keeper, Louis Cronin. Two tradesmen were also working there at the time.

As keepers on Fastnet, our official role in the race was to maintain radio listening watch and to pass on any messages that were not being acknowledged by the intended receiver, as well as providing an aid to navigation by keeping the lighthouse beam shining.

As was traditional, once the participating yachts came into view, the Fastnet keepers would note their sail numbers and times of passing. Then, we would radio the information to the keepers at Mizen Head and they would telephone the data to the race organisers in Cowes, as well as to the *Cork Examiner*.

On that fateful Saturday in August, 306 yachts, with 3,000 competitors on board, from 22 countries, set sail from Cowes to begin the race. Weather conditions were ideal, with reasonable winds and calm seas. The BBC radio shipping forecast broadcast at 1.55 p.m. predicted, 'South-westerly winds, force 4 to 5, increasing to force 6 to 7 for a time.'

On the following Sunday morning, a dense fog closed in around Fastnet Rock. Rolling fog is a regular occurrence in that particular part of the coastline, especially if warm southerly winds are present.

On Fastnet, we issued weather reports to the Irish Meteorological Service every four hours, as an aid to their forecast. We gave the direction and strength of the wind, the air temperature, the rise and fall of the sea, as well as the amount of cloud in the sky. Only certain lighthouses provided this service. Also, at Fastnet, as well as at every lighthouse, we recorded weather conditions every hour for a fog watch and also every four hours.

When keepers signed off from a watch, they recorded the barometrical pressure, by noting whether it was high or low and by measuring the pressure in inches. On that Sunday, conditions were still good and ideal for the race.

On Monday, the fog cleared at 8.45 a.m. and the wind registered at southerly force 3. A woman named Mrs Good rang Fastnet Rock and asked me if she could come out to the rock by boat to watch the yachts circling the lighthouse. I warned her against it, as the wind had begun to freshen and the fog had cleared very quickly. Both conditions together indicated that the weather was about to change for the worst. Around 2.00 p.m., the wind shifted to south-south-east and increased to strength 4.

On Fastnet, we kept a close eye out for the yachts. About 4.00 p.m., as the wind shifted again to southerly force 4, the first of the vessels sailed into view and began to round the lighthouse. These yachts were huge and rated among the biggest of the fleet. They would have gained great ground as the freshening, south-easterly winds would have blown them forward and increased their pace.

As evening approached, the winds grew stronger. Our radio on Fastnet broke down. Luckily, an Irish Lights helicopter happened to be in Castletownbere and delivered a new radio to the rock, which was a radio telephone transmitter and receiver, in medium frequency, with a range of about 150 miles. While we awaited the new radio, we kept contact with the keepers on Mizen Head by telephone. Once the new radio arrived, we resumed radio contact with them straight away.

At 6.00 p.m., the wind shifted back to south-south-east and increased to force 6. A small, wooden, pleasure craft sailed out to Fastnet from Crookhaven to observe the yachts rounding Fastnet. The weather deteriorated rapidly and the wind strengthened. The sea raged and the rise and fall of the waves varied between 10 and 15 feet. Standing on the balcony of the Fastnet, I watched the small vessel for hours through my binoculars as it tried to take shelter on the rough sea. It was the only boat in sight. Since the passing of the first, large, race yachts, no other yacht had reached the Fastnet, which suggested that the remainder lagged far behind the leaders.

I continued to watch the small boat as it struggled on the sea. At first, it sailed under the Fastnet. Then, it drifted eastwards and headed towards Cape Clear Island, about three miles east of the Fastnet. But I was unsure if the craft was actually in difficulty, as it seemed to be keeping its head up against the weather. At 8.00 p.m., the wind increased to gale force 8 and it began to rain. Conditions deteriorated further.

At 10.00 p.m., the lights of the small vessel disappeared and the boat went out of sight. I became alarmed and immediately contacted Baltimore Lifeboat by telephone. The secretary's wife, Eileen Bushe, answered the call. She listened attentively to my concern. When I requested to have the lifeboat launched to search for the vessel, she said that it was already on the ocean, as a boat with an RTÉ press crew on board had failed to return to Schull at the expected time. On that fateful night, the members of the lifeboat crew who took to the seas were: Christy Collins, coxswain;

Pat Harrington, acting second coxswain; Michael O'Connell, mechanic; John O'Regan, assistant mechanic; Noel Cottrell, second assistant mechanic; Paul O'Regan; Dan Cahalane; and Kieran Cotter. Although the lifeboat *The Robert* scoured the ocean in search of the small vessel, it failed to find the missing boat.

As the lifeboat began making its way back to Crookhaven, some of the racing yachts sailed into view near Fastnet. By now, the storm was raging and the sea thrashed 55 feet high against the entrance door of the lighthouse. We locked up and battened down all our storm doors. We had no fear for our own safety, as we had experienced much harsher conditions in winter time. But we were now becoming increasingly concerned for the 3,000 competitors in the race, many of whom had small vessels, no radios and may have been inexperienced in sailing on enormous seas in stormy weather.

In the lighthouse, we had an Aldis lamp, which we used for Morse code by light at night and which could throw a bright beam over a distance of several miles. Now, we used it to read the sail numbers on the yachts as they rounded Fastnet. We sent the information to Mizen Head lightkeepers by radio and they forwarded it to Cowes by telephone.

Sometimes, when we shone the Aldis lamp on the yachts, a massive wave battered against the rock and blotted out our view, allowing us to see only a huge volume of water, sweeping forcefully right over the rock, leaving merely the top of the tower visible. We took no notice of the onslaught and continued to shine our light on the yachts.

At 11.00 p.m., conditions worsened. The sea rose higher and higher and battered against the rock at a height of 80 feet. The wind reached strong gale force 9. As the yachts continued to round the Fastnet, the crews battled hard to control their boats. The number of people on each yacht varied, depending on the size of the boat. On average, crews probably numbered between six and nine.

At midnight, the wind shifted again from south-south-east to southerly and increased to storm force 10. At 15 minutes past midnight, we started sounding the fog horn. To the mariners struggling for their lives on the tempestuous sea, its high-pitched blare must have sounded like a siren from hell.

On Fastnet, we listened to the radio on the distress frequency 2182kcs, to which all ships at sea are constantly tuned. Many yachts were in serious difficulty. Some were capsizing in the far-off distance, east of Fastnet. But many of the boats had no radio and no means of communication. They could only rely on other nearby vessels to report their distress.

On the distress frequency, some of the yachts between the Scilly Isles and Fastnet broadcasted a May Day Relay, which is a call for help for another capsized yacht. But many of the mariners who saw their competitors in difficulty were unable to assist them. Being at the mercy of the mighty sea and violent storm, they too would have capsized if they had stopped to help.

As we listened on Fastnet to the distress frequency, we picked up information from many of the struggling crews, not only about their own yachts, but also about other boats. We heard that people were clinging to the sides of their boats on the mountainous ocean, that many yachts were turned upside down, while other boats showed no sign of life. Some vessels were rolling 360 degrees. Even the world-class yachts were in serious trouble, with some pitch-poling, flipping end over end. Although the voices of the distressed mariners sounded agitated, they communicated their cries for help with clarity. They gave the name of their yacht and sail number, as well as an accurate description of their position and the state of their vessel.

When we shone the Aldis lamp on a yacht, it lit up the entire deck and surrounding water, which was in extreme turmoil and breaking high over the decks of the yachts. Crew members were struggling to walk on heaving decks, trying to keep their balance, as they strove to trim their sails, to control their boats, while the person at the helm tried to turn the boat. Many of the yachts were only a quarter of a mile east of Fastnet. As they attempted to round the lighthouse, they kept a long way west of the rock, to avoid being foundered. But their task was tough, as they were at the mercy of the vicious, swirling wind and tumultuous sea.

At 1.35 a.m., a Cork yacht named *Regardless*, owned by Cork man Ken Rohan, put out a distress call when it lost its carbon fibre rudder. The yacht was positioned about three miles south-east of Fastnet Rock and had been fancied to win its class in the race until it got into difficulty. As the boat lost control, the crew lowered its sails and streamed ropes from the stern to keep the yacht's head onto the seas. The southerly wind continued to lash at force 10.

After spending hours searching for the small missing vessel, the Baltimore lifeboat, *The Robert*, which had begun its route to Crookhaven, set off west to save *Regardless*. The yacht had been drifting north-north-west. On seeing the Fastnet light, the lifeboat crew took their bearing from it. They knew they were south-east of the lighthouse, probably three or four miles away, but could not be certain of the exact distance. At the time, navigation equipment was unreliable and the crew had to rely on a Radio Direction Finding, which is a navigation system used to identify a radio source. As there were at least 15 yachts in the area at the time, battling against the storm, it was almost impossible for the lifeboat crew to distinguish one yacht from another and to identify *Regardless*. By then, the Irish naval ship, the *LE Deirdre*, was standing by the yacht in distress, as it happened to be patrolling the area. Its presence helped the lifeboat locate *Regardless*. Once the lifeboat arrived, *Regardless* cast off its ropes, to avoid fouling her propellers, and *The Robert* began towing her towards Baltimore, with a crew of nine on board. Along the way, the tow was lost five times.

Only yards off Fastnet, close to the rock, we could see Hugh Coveney's yacht, *Golden Apple of the Sun*. Ron Holland, the designer of the yacht, was among its crew, as well as Scotsman and three-time Olympic yachting medallist Rodney Pattisson. The yacht sliced its way through a narrow passage of water that opened up after a wave struck the rock, fell back again and met up with an incoming wave. The vessel was so near the lighthouse that we could almost reach out and touch it. Years before, when I was lobster fishing with Pat Joe Harrington, our neighbour at Galley Head, he explained to me about this calm strip of water, saying an old fisherman had told him that if skilled sailors kept their wits about them in stormy conditions, they could sail on this narrow channel, as it was known to be a safe passage.

By now, the vicious sea was breaking up high over the top of Fastnet Rock, hammering at a height of 90 to 100 feet and causing the tower to sway. Building material tied on to the side of the cliff, about 80 feet up the rock, was ripped asunder. At that stage, I was due to go off duty, to try and get a few hours sleep. Knowing that we had a long night ahead and that we needed to be on top of the job, it was important that each lightkeeper took a nap, even if only for a few hours. As I lay in my bunk bed, I could hear stones rolling below on the ocean floor and banging relentlessly against the tower. The southerly wind continued to batter at storm force 10.

After I resumed watch at 2.00 a.m., a group of four yachts came into view. Due to the strength of the mighty ocean and storm force winds, they failed to turn at the Fastnet. Instead, they were forced to head for Crookhaven, to turn their yachts near land. Many of the other yachts abandoned the race and veered to ports along the south coast of Ireland, such as Baltimore, Ballycotton, Cobh, Cork Harbour, Crosshaven and Kinsale, while some headed for Wales. *Finndabar*, owned by Patrick Jameson, a commissioner at Irish Lights, abandoned the race just off Kinsale, while *Morning*

Cloud, whose skipper was the former British prime minister Edward Heath, lost its rudder and headed for Cork Harbour. Later, Mr. Heath recalled his ordeal: 'It's an experience that I do not think anybody would want to go through again willingly. It was a raging sea with enormous waves and one of them picked us up and laid us on our side.'

In the early hours of the morning, we stopped reading the sail numbers, as we felt the powerful glare from the Aldis lamp was blinding the crews and hindering their struggle. At 3.00 a.m., the wind shifted up to the west and continued up to storm force 10. The westerly wind hoisted the waves up to about 40 feet at sea and in excess of 100 feet on the rock.

All through the early morning hours, the race participants battled on, with the westerly wind still howling at storm force 10. Around 6.00 a.m., the wind shifted into the north-west. Shortly afterwards a massive search and rescue operation got underway, co-ordinated by the Shannon Rescue Co-ordination Centre and the Plymouth Rescue Control Centre. Over 4,000 rescuers were summoned, among them the Royal Navy; the Dutch Navy; the entire Irish Navy; tugs; tankers; trawlers, including French trawlers; commercial ships; a fleet of RAF helicopters and RAF Nimrod jets, Irish Sea Rescue Services; and lifeboats from RNLI England and the south coast of Ireland, including crews from Courtmacsherry, Youghal, Valentia, Dunmore East and Ballycotton, with *The Robert* continuing to play its part. Most of the rescuers would have been called in by British Coast Radio. The British Air Force flew over, having been summoned by Landsend Radio, a coast radio station set up to handle shipping telephone messages. They air lifted many of the crews in difficulty. By coincidence, the Irish Navy happened to be on patrol when the yachts got into difficulty and contacted their naval base at Haulbowline in County Cork to summon the rest of the fleet.

Many of the damaged vessels were escorted into ports, such as *Silver Apple*, which called for help after its steering broke, and was led into Cork Harbour by the *LE Deirdre*. The crew of *Alvina* took to a life raft and had a narrow escape, as their vessel smashed to bits shortly afterwards. Hugh Coveney and his entire crew were airlifted to safety by an RAF Lynx helicopter after the yacht's rudder snapped in colossal waves and the ten men on board squeezed into a life raft. The crew of *Hestrul ll* was also airlifted.

As day was breaking, I saw a small yacht, about 30 feet in length, come into view from the east, which was the direction from which many of the distress calls came. It had hoisted its storm jib, which is a very small sail on the bow. The yacht moved extremely fast. In an instant, it spun around and headed in the opposite direction, confirming yet again the powerlessness of the yachts against the storm. Eventually, the yacht was able to correct its course and round the Fastnet.

About 8.00 a.m., *The Robert* landed *Regardless* and its crew safely at Baltimore. Then it headed off to search for the 55-foot *Marionette* and its crew of twelve, which, like *Regardless*, had lost its rudder. The yacht gave its position as south-east of the Stag's, a few miles from Baltimore. By the time *The Robert* located *Marionette*, it had drifted 25 miles south of Galley Head lighthouse.

At 10.00 a.m., the wind began to decrease to strong gale force 9. In the next hour, the wind shifted to west-north-west and blew at force 8. Around 1.00 p.m., the wind dropped to force 7. At 3.00 p.m., it shifted to west and then fell further to force 6.

Midway between Land's End and Fastnet, at least 125 competitors, whose yachts had been caught up in Force 11 violent storm strength gusts, were picked up by rescuers.

On the mainland, Richard Bushe, the secretary of Baltimore Lifeboat, organised ambulances and arranged a supply of dry clothes for the survivors. The crew of *The Robert* had worked tirelessly and helped survivors for 36 hours non-stop, longer than any other lifeboat.

Back at Plymouth Harbour, worried relatives and friends of the sailors who had not returned stood on the pier, gazing far out to sea, over the waters of the English Channel, waiting anxiously for the return of their loved ones.

Gradually, the extent of the horrific disaster began to unfold. Sadly, 15 of the competitors had perished in the monstrous storm. Six of the lives were lost because safety harnesses broke. The remainder drowned or died from hypothermia. The deceased sailors were named as Paul Baldwin, Robin Bowyer, Sub Lieutenant Russell Brown, David Crisp, Peter Dorey, Peter Everson, Frank Ferris, William L. Fevre, John Puxley, Robert Robie, David Sheahan, Sub Lieutenant Charles Steavenson, Roger Watts, Gerrit Jan Williahey and Gerald Winks.

Of the 306 yachts in the race, 25 were sunk or disabled, among them *Magic*, *Polar Bear* and *Charioteer*. Abandoned yachts included *Allamader*, *Ariadne*, *Billy Bones*, *Bonaventure*, *Callirhaex 3*, *Fiestina Tertia*, *Gan*, *Kestel*, *Maligawa III*, *Tarantula*, *Trophy* and *Tiderace IV*.

One of the survivors, Matthew Sheahan, who was only seventeen at the time and a crew member on his father's yacht, *Grimalkin*, described losing his father in the storm: 'One of the crew had realised my father was in a very bad way and needed to get out from under the boat, and he had cut my father's safety harness to free him. As I stood up and looked up, I could see a body, face down in the water. We were drifting away from it. There was absolutely no question in my mind that it was my father. The worst thing was that he was upwind of the boat and the boat was drifting downwind. Had it been the other way round, we could have got the life raft or something to go downwind and help pick him up. But upwind in those conditions: impossible.' He also described the impact when the yacht capsized: 'We were thrown out of the boat. Sometimes it would just be rolled over onto its side and catapult the crew into the water. Other times it would roll completely over and come up the other way. Worse still was when it was pitch-poled, when the boat actually does a cartwheel. The bow ploughs into the wave in front and the back gets lifted up by another wave.' He added that the waves were the size of buildings.

Dónal McClement, a navigator with the Royal Air Force and skipper of a seven-man crew sailing in the RAF class-4 yacht, *Black Arrow*, recalled his ordeal: 'I made a decision about 2.00 a.m. that even if a boat was next to us, there was nothing we could do as we would be risking our boat and our crew in helping them. We saw flares going up so we knew people were in trouble but there was no way we could get to them. I was lucky that I had a crew that were very experienced and used to discipline and leadership. Others just didn't know what hit them.'

Over the coming days, Valentia Radio broadcasted the names and sail numbers of missing yachts. On Fastnet Rock, we checked our records to see if any of these were entered as having passed Fastnet. We were able to give the sail numbers of some of the yachts that passed and were still passing. However, our records were incomplete, as we had switched off the Aldis lamp in the early hours of Tuesday morning.

Following the disaster, the media spotlight focused on Fastnet Rock. Reggie, the principal keeper, was interviewed on RTÉ radio, during a 9.00 a.m. news broadcast, and gave a detailed description of the sea disaster.

Although the storm had erupted out of the blue, people were now pointing the finger and looking for someone to blame. Doubt was cast on the weather reports issued by the lightkeepers at Fastnet Rock. We submitted our weather reports in their entirety to the headquarters of the Commissioners of Irish Lights at Pembroke Street in Dublin. We were duly commended for our accuracy and received a letter of appreciation on behalf of the Commissioners of Irish Lights in September 1979 stating: 'I am pleased to convey their thanks and appreciation for observations and communications with the sea and air rescue services, which, in the best tradition of this Service, helped greatly the success of the sea and rescue operation in your area.'

The Royal Ocean Racing Club, which had organised the race, received heavy criticism, especially in relation to its failure to call off the race when the weather seriously deteriorated, as it was argued that many competitors kept on racing for the honour of the race, instead of running for a port. Together with the Royal Yachting Association, the Royal Ocean Racing Club immediately commissioned an official inquiry into the disaster. By setting up the inquiry rapidly, both organisations hoped to preempt any official government inquiry and to show that sailing was a sport that could govern itself responsibly. The inquiry cleared the Royal Ocean Racing Club of any blame.

In the aftermath, new regulations were introduced to limit the number of yachts competing in the Fastnet race to 300. Also, it became compulsory for all yachts to be equipped with a VHF radio and for safety harnesses to have a locking device. Qualifications for entry to the competition were also introduced. Furthermore, a new strapping to airlift seafarers in difficulty was developed, consisting of a strap for around the legs and a strap for around the waist. In 1983, restrictions on electronic navigational aids were lifted.

The Fastnet yacht race of 1979 left an indelible mark on my mind that remains to this very day. In the wake of the tragedy, I received many moving telephone calls, one of the most poignant being a call from Mrs Good, the woman I had advised not to sail to the rock. She phoned to thank me for the warning.

The tragedy stands as the worst offshore racing disaster and the largest rescue operation ever in peacetime Europe, while the weather conditions of the time were described as the deadliest storm in the history of modern sailing.

The winner of the 1979 race was *Tenacious*, designed by Sparkman and Stephens and owned and skippered by the American media mogul Ted Turner, who founded the cable news network CNN and was once married to the well-known actress Jane Fonda.

Years after the race tragedy, while I was on duty on Mizen Head during the Cork Dry Gin Round Ireland Challenge yacht race, I was having a cup of tea with members of an RTÉ outside-broadcast unit, who were waiting to film the yachts circling Mizen. When the conversation switched to the tragic Fastnet race of 1979, I told them about the little vessel I had watched for hours until its light disappeared. They said that they were the crew of that very vessel, as they had sailed to the Fastnet to film the race. They were unaware that *The Robert* had been launched to search for them. Their vessel had made its way safely back to Crookhaven. All of them survived.

8

Old Head of Kinsale

In the months following the Fastnet tragedy, I was transferred to the lighthouse at the Old Head of Kinsale, a County Cork landmark famous for being the nearest land point to the site where the *RMS Lusitania* sank in 1915. The original lighthouse had a cottage-type design, unique to Ireland, and burned an open, coal fire in a steel-framed basket on its roof. Its remains can still be seen today. The present lighthouse, which was the third built at the location, was first lit on 1 October 1853.

It was only when I started at the Old Head that I realised I was extremely fit. Of course this was due to the lay-out of the Fastnet, as the kitchen there was located at the top of the tower, while other facilities were located at the bottom, which meant it was necessary to climb up and down the entire lighthouse countless times each day.

Lightening was common at the Old Head. One evening, in the midst of a ferocious storm, I decided to shift my car, which I had parked outside the front door of the keepers' house. As I stepped outside, a flash of lightening struck the car, burned the paint on the bonnet and knocked off the number plate. Another flash damaged our wiring system, jumped all the fuses and ruined our radio transmitter.

Years later, when my twin brother Edmund worked at the Old Head, a gigantic wave burst in the back window of his house and floated all its contents. Luckily, he managed to get his family into their car and make a run for it. The same wave thrashed half-way up the lighthouse, burst in a window, cascaded down the steps and gushed out the door. It also smashed a boat into the back of a bus in Clonakilty.

Around 11.00 a.m. one morning, I spotted what appeared to be big puffs of smoke drifting on the water. I had never seen these before and immediately phoned the Irish naval base in Haulbowline, thinking that the navy might be carrying out gunnery practice in the area. My hunch was wrong and I later found out that massive whales were swimming along under the surface, never breaking it, but sending up huge gusts of air topped with sea spray.

Lobsters were plentiful in the waters around the Old Head. In my diving gear, I'd swim along the shore line and drop my pots into cracks and crevices. One day as I tried to swim with my lobster pots, the tide was so strong that it kept knocking me back and prevented me from laying them.

During my time at the Old Head, trade shipping was the only type of shipping in the area. Normally, the trade ships sailed along the south and south-west coast. Banana boats rated high among the passing vessels. A lot of the boats belonged to certified shipping companies. We got to know many of them, such as Manchester Liners, which were large vessels that shipped cargo to America. Some of the boats had sixteen derricks or more for loading and unloading the cargo. But in time, all of that changed when container ships became common.

Whenever I saw ships with several derricks, I thought of my father. In his early days, he had worked as an able-bodied seaman with the merchant navy and often recalled his life at sea. He told me about the many, big Sampson posts that stood up on the decks, with all the derricks on top, often as many as 15 or 16. As a ship neared a port, each derrick had to be painted and the ship had to be scrubbed from top to bottom to prevent the onset of rust. Once the ship docked, it was able to unload itself by using the derricks.

At the Old Head, as at every lighthouse, when springtime came along, painting became a priority. I jumped at the chance to paint the mast, as it meant sitting on a bosun's chair, which was a timber plank, with ropes going from the sides to the centre and running through a block. I painted the 30-foot mast, every inch of it, by sitting on that chair and swirling carefree around the mast, as if I was spinning on a merry-go-round. At the top of the mast, I took in the bird's eye view of the rugged cliffs and foamy waves as they rushed relentlessly towards the headland and I studied any vessels that sailed nearby, especially fishing trawlers, as many of them worked off the Old Head.

One night, when the Irish navy tried to arrest a trawler that was illegally fishing in the area, the fishing vessel brazenly put up a fight by facing the navy ship head-on and passing it at full speed. Straight away, the navy began firing tracer bullets from the stern of the ship, over the trawler, as a signal for the fishing vessel to stop. I could see a line of tracer shots hitting the water, leaving a glowing trace of fire behind, then rising vertically, high into the air. As the navy would turn its ship around, the trawler would face it again, head-on, and speed off for about a half-mile, with another line of bullets on its trail, then swerve around once more to further antagonise the navy ship. This continued for ages and sometimes the fishing vessel would duck in and out between other nearby fishing boats. While I was unable to wait for the outcome, I read a newspaper report soon after stating that a fishing trawler had been arrested off the Old Head for illegal fishing. At the time, most of the trawlers fished there for herring, which has always been under strict control, due to quotas.

As the Old Head was situated close to both Cork and Cross-haven, small yacht races were a common sight, especially in summer time. In the distance, the boats made a pretty picture, twinkling in the sunshine and flapping their snow-white sails as they gracefully glided along on the sparkling blue sea.

During the summer months, we had a constant flow of visitors to the Old Head. Even though the general public were forbidden access and the entrance gate was always locked, they still came. They climbed over the gate and wandered up the winding, one-mile path to the lighthouse, unhindered. We always turned a blind eye to the fact that they were not entitled to be there, chatted away with them and answered all their questions. Usually, they just looked around at the lighthouse and cliffs and then strolled back out again. But those who did ask questions were always captivated by the principal keeper, Eugene Gillen, who had a wealth of history on the Old Head, which he gladly shared. According to Eugene, in early Christian times the Old Head was a settlement area and its inhabitants deliberately lured ships in towards the rocks for the purpose of pilfering them. Even now, whenever the area is covered by melting snow, it's possible to see the ring of the settlement from the air.

Often, birds at the Old Head, especially manx shearwaters or storm petrels, crashed into the lantern and fell down into the yard or balcony. On finding them, we'd fling them high into the air and watch with delight as they flew away, fully recovered. Such accidents were rare on the western side of the Old Head, where the cliffs were extremely sheer and rose to a height of 180 feet. Those cliffs always reminded me of the Bull Rock, as they attracted similar birds, such as guillemots and razorbills.

For many years, goats roamed wild around the Old Head. When I had worked there previously as an SAK, we confined one of them and milked her every day. In years to come, the goat population there was exterminated because of in-breeding.

As change was part and parcel of life at the Old Head, so too my own personal life was moving in a different direction, as I had married shortly before being transferred to the Old Head, having become engaged while serving on the Fastnet, and I was now in the process of building my own house.

Even though I was born in Castletownbere, I always considered Galley Head as home, as my parents had lived at the Galley longer than at any other station and my father still worked there as the principal keeper. And so, I asked my former employer Matt O'Sullivan, who was still in the auctioneering business, to keep an eye out for a suitable site for me near the Galley. On Matt's recommendation, I ended up buying a lovely elevated eight-acre site, situated high above Rathbarry, a charming little village nestling within miles of Galley Head.

Once I started my house, I gave it my full attention and put all adventures and escapades on hold. Every morning, after coming off the 6.00 a.m. watch at the Old Head, I hopped on my Honda 50 and headed for Rathbarry to work on the building. Edmund acted as my right-hand man. Together, we sweated it out and did all the plumbing, carpentry and electrical work ourselves. Finishing the house became my priority.

In the midst of the building, after more than two years at the Old Head, I was transferred to Mizen Head lighthouse, near Fastnet Rock. I had previously worked for a month on the Mizen during my time as an SAK and felt very excited at the thought of returning. Little did I know then that it would be the last lighthouse on which I would serve as a lightkeeper and that my service would end much sooner than expected.

9

Mizen Head

A scenic island in west Cork, Mizen Head attracts 100,000 tourists annually. One of the island's most striking features is its spectacular, world-renowned, arched pedestrian footbridge, which connects the island's lighthouse to the mainland.

Built in 1909, almost 150 feet above the crashing waves of the Atlantic, and spanning more than 165 feet across a dramatic rock inlet, the original bridge was considered to be the longest reinforced concrete bridge of its type in Europe.

Also built in 1909, Mizen Head lighthouse operated mainly as a fog signal station. Its famous 99 steps run along a pathway to the rocky outcrop on which the station is located.

In 2011, the iconic Victorian bridge was replaced by an equally impressive bridge, constructed in reinforced concrete, using stainless steel, with a two-pin arch. Built at a cost of €1.8 million and funded by the local authority, Fáilte Ireland and Irish Lights, the new landmark bridge received much acclaim. Also, it renewed interest in the history of the lighthouse.

On 1 October 1959, a buoy lantern was erected at the point of the peninsula to illuminate the lighthouse, as the station had been unlit until then. The lighthouse depot stored an abundant supply of buoy lanterns, as these lamps were also used to light floating buoys, shipwrecks or points of danger. The light at Mizen had a character of two seconds on and two seconds off, with the range of the light being increased to 16 nautical miles on 10 October 1968.

As keepers on the Mizen, we lit the light manually and monitored its operation from the kitchen.

Our oil was delivered by road, fed into a tank at the top of the steps and then stored in tanks at the station for use in our standby generator. To obtain a supply of drinking water, we caught seepage from the nearby mountain in a catchment area. Having ensured that the water had no salt, we piped it through the handrails and stored it in a large, closed, concrete tank, high over the station.

The lighthouse used explosive fog signals until 1972, when explosive fog signals were discontinued. From the 1930s onwards, it was also used for Radio Direction Finding, which is an electronic navigation system used to identify the direction and strength of a radio source.

The radio beacon, or RB, which is known to the mariner as radio direction finding, is an electronic navigation system used by ships far out in the ocean to chart their position. During the 1930s, an RB was fitted at Mizen Head. A radio beacon transmits a continuous or periodic radio signal with limited information content, such as its identification or location, on a specified radio frequency. The radio beacon at Mizen operated on a signal that broadcasted in Morse code on the long wave frequency. Mizen identified itself by repeating the letters MZ three times, followed by a long, continuous dash. With their on-board Radio Direction Finder unit, ships at sea could tune into the signal being emitted from a lighthouse's RB to find the directional angle of its source relative to the ship. For example, if a ship sailing a few hundred miles out on the Atlantic knew its angle direction from Mizen Head, and repeated the process for an RB at another lighthouse, then transferred these readings to the Admiralty Chart by drawing lines corresponding to the ship's angle of direction from both lighthouses, the ship could then identify its position on the chart as being where both lines intersect.

Our radio beacon at Mizen had two pendulum clocks. We received our signal from the BBC and adjusted our pendulum clocks for the radio beacon by adding weights onto the pendulum or removing them. These signals covered what was known as the western approaches to Europe.

Mizen was grouped with five other stations: Barra Head in Scotland, Créac'h lighthouse in France, Round Island in the Isles of Scilly, Tory Island off Donegal and Eagle Island off Mayo. Each station transmitted for 55 seconds. Then a five-second pause ensued before the next broadcast began. Barra Head started its transmission bang on the hour. Mizen was fourth in line and went on air at three minutes past the hour. Timing had to be spot on. If timing failed to be 100 per cent accurate, one station might transmit on top of another, causing a ship to lose vital information and disrupting the individual timing for all stations, often for a few hours.

Our radio beacon mast stood on four porcelain insulators. Its earthing was poor. During stormy conditions, when the sea spray washed over the rock, the radio transmitting signal would cut across the insulators, go to ground through the lightening conductors and consequently reduce the range of our radio beacon direction finding signal. To wash off the sea spray, we'd throw fresh water on the insulators after our transmission finished. But we had to be extremely careful to avoid being electrocuted. Once the sea spray was washed away, the range of the signal dramatically increased again.

Later, Irish Lights purchased some land from a neighbouring farmer, Denis Downey, on the side of a hill outside the lighthouse. We erected two big, steel, radio beacon masts at the top of the hill, with a transmission aerial between them and a spider's web of earth wires, sunk deep into the ground beneath the transmitters. Due to its location, the new aerial gave an excellent transmission, increased the range of our signal to about 300 miles and ended the need to wash the insulators.

As well as conducting a radio watch, we kept a visual watch on the sea, as did keepers at all lighthouses. We logged the names and numbers of passing ships, as well as their times of passing. The data recorded at Mizen Head proved especially useful, as customs officials and the gardaí regularly requested information from our observations. We built up a great working relationship with them, especially during the Northern Ireland troubles of the 1980s, when they had to keep a close eye out for drug trafficking and arms smuggling. Once customs received information from the international criminal police organisation, Interpol, about the departure of a suspect vessel, the customs officers would immediately contact us to ask us to keep an eye out for its passing, as they were never sure of its destination. At all times, we were on the alert, constantly on the look-out for anything suspicious.

At Mizen, we also had a racon, which was fitted to the lighthouse in July 1968. A racon is a radar responder beacon that shows up on the radar screen of a ship, in a Morse code identification signal, measuring two miles on the monitor. The lighthouses' identification signal was received in Morse code, two letters representing each station, for example MZ for Mizen Head, or GL for Eagle Island. The racon was necessary because when the radar scanner on the ship passed a lighthouse, the station showed up as a dot on the screen and this identified it. Observation of the racon was unnecessary, other than to ensure that it operated correctly.

In the kitchen, we had a little speaker connected to the racon. It gave us a squelching sound of a ship if a ship's radar was interrogating our racon. A very loud emission signalled that the ship was extremely close.

The radar scanner on a ship emits a signal and when that signal bounces off any object, it returns and shows up as a small dot on the ship's radar screen. When a ship's signal rebounded from the

Mizen, our racon sent a signal back with the returning signal from the ship and it showed up on the ship's screen as a long flash, measuring two miles, and identifying the position of the lighthouse.

Before the Global Positioning System was introduced in 1982, a private company named Decca developed the Decca Navigator System, a hyperbolic, low frequency radio navigation system that was first used in June 1944 to guide ships leading the D-Day invasion through the mine fields off the north coast of France. The DNS system was the brainchild of an American engineer named William J. O'Brien and its first marine trials were conducted between Anglesey and the Isle of Man.

Decca chains of navigation were set up in all the principal shipping areas around the world, with an estimated 200,000 users in Europe alone. An Bord Iascaigh Mhara, the agency responsible for developing the Irish marine fishing and aquaculture industries, managed Decca's Irish chain 7D. When Decca found itself under financial strain, the General Lighthouse Authorities assumed responsibility for the system in February 1987, at the expense of the General Lighthouse Fund.

In comparison to other land-based, low frequency radio navigation systems, the DNS had certain disadvantages. In contrast to long-range systems, such as Loran-C – a radio directional finding signal with a range of 1,200 miles – DNS had a short range. Also, it was expensive to run, as it used low-power transmitters and needed 24 transmitters to provide coverage for Irish and British waters. On average, running the system cost £3.5 million annually.

At midnight, on 31 March 2000, the General Lighthouse Authorities ceased to operate the DNS system and An Bord Iascaigh Mhara stopped its transmission on 19 May 2000.

Before the GPS was completed, we carried out tests at Mizen for many radio transmitter companies to pick up Loran-C. Several firms set up their radio equipment at Mizen Head and tried to pick up a radio signal from as far away as possible. Some managed to pick up a signal from the Arctic Circle by using a five-foot, fibre-glass whip aerial. Obtaining such a signal proved that it would be possible to get tremendous range into a signal going across the Atlantic.

Later, Irish Lights was asked to erect a mast at Loop Head to transmit one of these signals. However, various groups of people opposed the proposed mast due to fears of radiation and also because the type of mast required was being used by the French for military purposes. Some time later, the mast was erected in the south of England.

In 1982, the Department of Defence in America launched the first of a constellation of 24 satellites that today enable the operations of the Global Positioning System, known as GPS. Once the programme was completed, about ten years later, it provided the most accurate navigation system in the world, as all of the satellites operated perfectly on time. For example, if one of the satellites was positioned directly over us at noon, it would be in exactly the same place on the following day at five minutes past midday and at ten minutes past noon the next day, consequently losing a single revolution annually.

At Mizen, as the millennium drew near, we feared that our electronic equipment might not switch over automatically from the year 1999 to 2000, but we need not have worried.

Although the GPS was intended primarily for military purposes, the general public was allowed to use it. Due to the possibility that GPS might be used for terrorist activity, the system featured an error, or selected availability, programme.

As surveillance was central to our duties at Mizen, accuracy was vital at all times and so we installed a differential GPS. This signalled the end of our radio beacon, as it had become outdated.

When a ship is travelling, it takes its bearing from the moving satellite. However, as Mizen was a fixed station, we were able to read the satellite's position and triangulate the information to the ship, thereby allowing the ship's computer to pick up our differential signal and make the necessary compensations. Such accuracy proved especially useful for oil exploration.

In the waters around the Mizen, ships regularly carried out seismic testing, which is a study of waves of energy that move through the earth in the wake of an earthquake, explosion or some other occurrence that creates low-frequency, acoustic energy. To conduct seismic testing, a ship towed a cable two miles in length for about 15 miles. The captain had to be 100 per cent certain of the ship's position. If the captain was in any doubt, the cable had to be hauled in immediately and the procedure would have to start all over again once the captain identified the ship's exact position. As each effort cost about £10,000, it was easy to understand the value of being able to establish an accurate position on the first attempt.

After some time, the American Department of Defence removed the selection availability, making the GPS accurate to several feet.

At Mizen Head, we always welcomed any technological developments that enhanced our work. Yet we were unaware that, in years to come, technology would advance to such an extent that the lightkeeper would become obsolete.

10

A People Apart

Being stationed at Mizen Head meant I was only 50 miles from Rathbarry and still able to nip over and back there during the day to work on the house. I swapped my Honda 50 for an old Hillman Hunter and shoved in a diesel engine, as well as a gear box. The old banger became my pride and joy, even though I probably spent more time trying to keep it together than driving it.

When I did spend some leisure time at Mizen, I often climbed to the top of the nearby mountain and soaked up the panoramic views, with Dunmanus Bay stretching lazily to my left and Rock Island to my right, showing off the jewel in its crown, Crookhaven lighthouse. I could pick out the remains of ancient potato ridges on the fields and stone huts where people had lived until the famine. Most of the huts have deteriorated or collapsed but their outline is still there. I often wondered what life must have been like at Mizen before the famine, when the area boasted a much bigger population and families survived on small holdings. But apart from being curious about the past, I also wanted to get to know those living in the locality and to make the most of my time among them.

The Mizen Head Cliff and Rescue Team gave me the perfect chance to make new friends and to learn cliff climbing and rescue techniques. And so I became one of its most ardent members. Under the guidance of Captain Dave O'Shiel, I began a strict, repetitive training programme of learning various skills, such as abseiling.

During training one evening, as I abseiled down a cliff on the end of a rope, I found myself moving over an overhang and being suspended in mid-air by the rope. Despite all my years of climbing, I had rarely relied on a rope for my safety. My father's words of wisdom came ringing in my ears once again, reminding me to rely always on my hands and feet. But that was impossible now, as I hung on, dangling in mid-air. Having to depend on a rope at that point, rather than on my hands and feet, scared the daylights out of me and filled me with insecurity and serious concern for my safety. If I wanted to continue, I would have to abandon my habit of self-reliance and develop confidence in the rope. Knowing it was the only way to master the skill of abseiling, I yielded and descended safely to the bottom of the cliff.

Training as a team, we abseiled all the local cliffs, from Goleen out to Baltimore. We trained in first aid and lifted volunteer casualties up and down the sides of cliffs on a stretcher. The team spirit was strong, so strong that we formed life-long friendships with each other, never to be broken. Even on my month off, I'd drive back to the Mizen once a week to train and meet up with the gang. Eventually, we were all officially certified to carry out cliff rescue by stretcher. Later, many of the cliff rescue teams around the coast became known as the Irish Marine Emergency Service, and the Irish Coast Guard.

Apart from forming close bonds with the rescue team, I fell in easily with the rest of the locals, all of whom were lovely, easy-going people and showed great respect for the lightkeepers. I got to know many of them by popping into the pubs in Goleen or the hotel in Barleycove and by attending Mass on Sundays with the principal keeper Reggie Sugrue, who sat beside me in my old banger, as we drove along the winding, country roads.

Many of the locals were fishermen and farmers, among them Denis Downey, the neighbouring farmer from whom Irish Lights had bought some hilly ground for the erection of the radio beacon masts. Denis and I became great pals and I spent many happy hours working on his tractors and doing electrical jobs around the farm. A private company erected a special, direction finding radio beacon on his land for oil exploration. It radiated in every direction and its mast rose high in the sky, to a height of 300 feet. A huge amount of stays held it in place and anchored it securely to the ground. Denis had a heart of gold. As we had no area on the cliff for vegetation, he ploughed and prepared part of one of his fields near the lighthouse for us. We ended up having a plentiful supply of vegetables every day, as we grew carrots, parsnips, turnips, onions and cabbage there. All the keepers shared the garden, which meant it was constantly weeded and always well maintained.

Apart from enjoying the company of the locals, I was privileged to meet many interesting visitors to the lighthouse, among them the actor John Cowley, who was best known for his role as Tom Riordan in the popular television drama *The Riordans*. John visited with a group of nuns from the convent in Rosscarbery. His real-life, warm persona seemed exactly the same as his genial on-screen character, so much so that the other keepers and I almost felt as if we were taking part in an episode of the series.

We had the honour too of welcoming the apostolic nuncio Dr Gaetano Alibrandi to the lighthouse. Like John Cowley, he also came in the company of nuns.

Other famous visitors to the lighthouse included John Guinness – the millionaire banker and company director who served as both a commissioner and chairman of Irish Lights – and his wife Jennifer. While her husband spoke with us, Mrs Guinness enthusiastically scanned the pages of the visitors' book. When she spotted the names of some of her ancestors who had served as commissioners with Irish Lights, she lifted her head and excitedly told her husband of her findings. It was obvious that they had a very loving relationship and Mr Guinness gave her his full attention each time she spoke, as if she was the only person in the room. A fellow keeper, whose girlfriend was their maid, happened to be in the Guinness house in Howth one night as Mrs Guinness walked down the stairway, dressed in her finery for an evening out. He said she was the most beautiful woman he had ever seen. Shockingly, in April 1986, a gang led by John Cunningham from Ballyfermot, who had strong connections with the John Gilligan trafficking gang, kidnapped Mrs Guinness from her home. Cunningham's gang demanded a ransom of £2 million but released Mrs Guinness and gave themselves up after a five-hour siege at a house in south Dublin. In 1996, while serving the final year of his sentence for the kidnapping, Cunningham escaped from Shelton Abbey open prison in County Wicklow and fled to Amsterdam. Years later, after being sentenced in the Netherlands for drug trafficking, he was extradited back to Ireland, where he served out the remainder of his sentence for the kidnapping.

One Christmas, my family came to the Mizen to spend the holiday period with me. As my three children, Deirdre, Teresa and Aidan, were all under the age of five, I took great care to protect them and dared not let them step outside the door of the lighthouse. On Christmas morning, Deirdre rose first and ran around excitedly, looking for Santa's presents. When she failed to find them, she sobbed that he must have forgotten to come. I assured her that the light at the top of the lighthouse had been flashing all night and that there was no way he would have flown by on his sleigh without calling. Together, we searched and eventually found the toys, well hidden by Santa in some nook or cranny.

Every Christmas without fail, John Gore-Grimes, one of the new commissioners of Irish Lights, dropped in with a bottle of whiskey for the keepers. John was a close friend of John Guinness and sadly witnessed his sudden death on Snowdon, when they were walking together. Over the years John Gore-Grimes visited the lighthouse frequently while staying at his holiday home in Durrus. His agility, strength and adventurous spirit never failed to amaze me and he would scale down the cliff with ease, with his heavy diving gear attached, and scramble back up again without a bother. Out of the blue one summer, he invited me to go diving with him. We dived to a depth of about 95 feet, right down to the rocky bottom of the sea, where much of the sea bed was covered in seaweed. A passing lobster took our fancy and we chased him. His two antennas stretched out ahead, threatening us. To distract him, we danced our fingers in front of him. But, as we attempted to seize him by the back, he swam backwards away from us and shot off into the distance.

During my nine years at Mizen Head, I always took great interest in everyone who visited the rock and I enjoyed the company of my fellow keepers too, some of whom were extremely gifted with their hands, as were many of the lightkeepers all around the Irish coast.

11

Pastimes

As a lightkeeper, it was important to have a hobby to pass the time, especially as the duty rota usually entailed four hours on and eight hours off and many keepers were stranded on rock stations. Sundays were especially long and boring, as keepers finished most of the maintenance work on weekdays, such as taking the lights apart and re-assembling them, or checking that the engines and fog signals remained in good working order. For any lightkeepers on a rock who failed to detach themselves from shore life and occupy their free time, the lighthouse became like a prison. But most of the lads adapted well. Many whiled away their spare time by reading or making things by hand, usually for the tourist market.

Some made key rings with an Irish emblem attached, such as a harp or a shamrock. Others made shell vases, shell lamps, Celtic crosses, woollen mats, rugs, and shillelagh walking sticks, carved from blackthorn, with straight or knob grips, and fancy knots at both ends. They painted the canes black and glossed them with spirit varnish. Most of the walking sticks were made to order and later sold to tourists, mainly in souvenir shops, or at Cork and Shannon airports. Many of the lightkeepers collected glass bottles in various shapes and sizes. They coated the bottles in cement, decorated them with sea shells and turned them into lamps.

One guy was a perfectionist and always on the look-out to acquire a new skill. At Power Head, he took up bait fishing on a beach and would spend a full day at a time perfecting his method. He'd put the bait onto a hook, usually lug worm. Then, bass or some other fish off the beach would eat it and get caught in the hook. He became gifted at knitting and crochet. He knitted jumpers and cardigans, including Aran sweaters with intricate stitches, and crocheted delicate, white and cream, lace table mats. Another lightkeeper was a talented cook and spent his leisure time making mouth-watering, caramel chocolates and iced biscuits.

Games such as cards, draughts and chess rated among the most popular hobbies. Some of the keepers played radio chess. To play radio chess, a lightkeeper on one station played against a lightkeeper on another station, by calling out every move over the radio to each other. As well as making model ships and weapons, playing radio chess became one of my favourite leisure pursuits. I had learned to play chess years before, when one of my younger brothers, Jimmy, taught me while I was laid up at home with scarlet fever. Jimmy, who had joined Irish Lights for a short spell before going to sea as an engineer, was an expert at chess, top class.

One of my first opponents was Gerry O'Brien, who was stationed at Roancarrig Lighthouse while I was on the Bull. Usually, our games lasted for days. The more I played him, the more my game improved, as I learned from him every time.

Often, the other keepers stood at my shoulder as I played, keeping an eye on the game, soaking up the tension, nodding their heads in agreement if I made a wise move, or sighing in disbelief if I messed up. When my opponent spoke on the radio to declare his move, they listened attentively and tried to detect any nervousness in his voice. They came and went, checking up on me in between carrying out their duties. But they never interrupted me, as they knew the importance of concentration. Sometimes, they placed bets on who would win. Often, the outcome affected their mood, even though for them it was never about the money, but more about the honour of the rock. While I was okay, I knew I could be better, maybe even as good as my brother Jimmy.

As a player, Jimmy was streets ahead of me. He always kept his cool and could beat the best of them, among them Artie Linnane, a fellow lightkeeper who later became a trainee instructor. I took on Artie time and time again. The best I could do was to win only every second game, no more. That got to me. Then one day, Artie happened to tell me that the only person who could beat him every time was my brother Jimmy.

When Jimmy and I met up at home on our time off, I asked him to tell me how I could hammer Artie. Jimmy's advice was simple, 'The only way to beat Artie is to spend longer than him thinking out your next move.'

On returning to the rock, I resumed my play with Artie, eager to put Jimmy's tactics to the test. I now had the ammunition. All it required was patience. Lo and behold it worked and I knocked Artie off his pedestal and put an end to his victories.

Whether playing radio chess or making model ships and weapons, I always tried to keep myself occupied, no matter what. One night at the Old Head, to pass away the time, I ended up fooling around with the resident mouse at the keeper's house. He had eaten a perfectly shaped hole into the skirting board in the kitchen and now had access to the entire house. In between watch duty one night, I spotted him peeping out of the gap. He glanced all around, as if he was standing at his own front door watching the traffic pass by. I waited until he crept back inside the hole. Then I cut a strand of wire and made a snare that would slip easily around his neck when caught. I fastened one end on to an ESB junction box.

Two hours later, I heard a racket under the kitchen table. On investigation, I found the mouse dancing around in the noose. I picked up one end of the wire and disconnected it. Then I put the mouse into a glass milk bottle on the kitchen table and decided to have some fun with him. I watched him twirl around as I twisted the bottle in various directions and threw in different bits for him to catch. Then the resident cat appeared. He tried and tried again to put his claw down the neck of the bottle but failed to reach the mouse. In the end, he gave up and fell asleep beside the bottle. By then, I had tired of watching the mouse and my patience was running out. I laid the bottle on its side and woke up the cat. He pushed his forearm into the bottle but still couldn't catch the mouse. Just as he dozed off again, the mouse ran out of the bottle and sprinted across the floor. As he dashed under the footboard of the table, the cat sprang, cleared the footboard, jumped into mid-air, landed on top of the mouse and did what he had been trying to do all night.

At Mizen Head, fellow lightkeeper Cíarán Ó Briain, known affectionately as Maverick, sheeted the walls of the lighthouse with paintings he created during his leisure time. A self-taught, natural artist, the extent of his talent astounded me, as he painted works of art that varied from scenery, to still-life and portrait. Once while we were chatting, he casually carved out a mirror image of me on a bar of soap. An RTÉ television crew filmed him for the traditional Irish crafts series *Hands* as he painted the Ballycotton lifeboat sailing out to sea. In just 30 minutes, he produced a masterpiece.

Another fellow keeper, Raymond Wickham from Wexford, spent his spare time crafting sailing ships, which he then inserted into a glass bottle. Visitors to the station marvelled at his ability to fit a ship into a bottle, especially as the neck of the bottle was narrower than the ship. Often, I stood over him as he worked, just as I'd stood at my father's side, when he made or mended shoes, and Raymond explained his craft to me. First, he made part of the hull of the ship by sliding a piece of timber into a glass bottle and gluing it onto the centre. Usually, he used a triangular Dimple whiskey bottle or one branded Teacher's. Then he carved out the shape of the rest of the timber hull, snipped three masts and made sails from white paper. He cut thread for the rigging, glued the sails to timber spars and attached the spars to the masts, which he hinged at the bottom, onto the deck, with all the rigging in place. He twisted the sails around the masts, lowered them onto the hull and twisted the lot into the shape of the handle of a fork, so that it would slip easily through the neck of the bottle. Working through the neck of the bottle, with a long, narrow, steel pin, like a needle with a hook, he glued the ship's hull onto the prepared base inside. Then, when he pulled each thread of rigging out through the bow of the ship, all of the masts stood up. He arranged the sails and glued the rigging in place. Once the glue dried, he trimmed the sails with a long, narrow blade and corked the bottle.

The mentality of gifted artists like Cíarán and Raymond enthralled me, as they seemed to take a different perspective on life to the rest of us, especially when it came to solving problems. I enjoyed listening to them talk, as they always adopted a positive outlook, no matter what. In their eyes, life seemed so much simpler and straight-forward. Nothing was insurmountable.

Although most lightkeepers switched off totally from their work during leisure time, while on duty their focus stayed firmly on those riding the seas.

12

On the Ocean Wave

One afternoon, when the wind blew in from the east, the air stream gusting off the land calmed the seas close to the rocks. When the other assistant keeper noticed a ship sailing in close to the rocks north of Mizen, he called the ship's captain and advised him that he was gliding in to very shallow ground. Foolishly, the captain took offence and in a cocky tone replied, 'I know where I'm going.' His failure to heed the warning alerted us straight away. We noted the name of the vessel and reported the ship to the customs authorities in Bantry. When the customs officials checked the background of the ship, they found that it had a history of drug trafficking. As a result, both customs and gardaí placed a watch on the ship. As lightkeepers, we had no further involvement. On the following morning, custom officials boarded the suspectable ship but found all was well.

One summer during the Cork Dry Gin Round Ireland Challenge yacht race, one of its participants, Patrick Jameson – an experienced race competitor who had survived the Fastnet race of 1979, as well as a commissioner of Irish Lights and a member of the well-known family that produces Jameson whiskey – contacted me by VHF radio. Along with the other yachts taking part in the race, his boat had become becalmed as the wind had ceased, leaving him stranded about six miles south-east of Mizen Head. He asked me to phone his wife and let her know his position. Over the next few days, as the yachts continued to sit on the waters, I phoned Mrs Jameson often and kept her up-to-date. At that stage, nobody had finished the race.

In Wicklow, the competition's organisers had been monitoring the progress of the yachts since the race began and they contacted me to request the times and sail numbers of the boats that passed Mizen lighthouse.

The yachts remained stranded for a few days. But they were never in any danger, as weather conditions were ideal and the crews had an adequate supply of food and drink on board. Eventually, the winds freshened from the west and the yachts began to make progress once again, sailing away west in the sunshine. Naturally, Mrs Jameson had been very concerned for her husband's well-being while he was marooned and she wrote me a lovely letter to thank me for communicating with both herself and Mr Jameson during his ordeal.

In September 1984, the FBI notified the Irish security service that a cargo of arms and ammunition was being shipped from Boston across the Atlantic by an American vessel, the *Valhalla*, as a consignment for the Irish Republican Army, with the intention of transferring it onto an Irish fishing trawler off the south-west in international waters, where Irish security forces had no authority.

At the naval base on Haulbowline Island, under the direction of Inspector Eric Ryan, a detailed plan of action was put in place to intercept the illegal shipment at sea. The anti-terrorist group included gardaí, naval personnel and three ships, the *LE Deirdre*, *LE Emer* and *LE Aisling*.

Following surveillance operations, the gardaí identified a Fenit-based trawler named the *Marita Ann* as the transfer vessel. As soon as the *Marita Ann* left the port of Dingle on 26 September to keep her appointment, the naval ships sailed out from Haulbowline with gardaí on board. The crew of the *Marita Ann* were unaware that they were under constant observation and that the voyage of the gun-running *Valhalla* was being closely monitored by international agencies.

Late on the night of 27 September, the *Marita Ann* positioned herself alongside the *Valhalla*, about 124 miles west of Ireland, in an area of shallow waters known as Porcupine Bank, a raised area of seabed lying between the deep waters of Porcupine Seabight and Rockall Trough. As the illicit cargo of arms and ammunition was transferred on to the *Marita Ann*, the entire operation was watched by a KHII spy satellite as it orbited the earth.

Off the Kerry coast, the blacked-out Irish naval ships waited patiently for the *Marita Ann* to enter Irish waters. Based on vital British intelligence data, the captain of the *LE Emer*, Lieutenant Commander Brian Farrell, had been able to pin-point the precise course of the *Marita Ann* and to plot the exact point of interception.

By midnight, the *Marita Ann* was positioned about 1,800 yards inside Irish territorial waters. Concealed by the Skellig rocks, the *LE Emer* moved in speedily on the targeted vessel.

During the early hours of Saturday 29 September, in heavy seas, within a half mile of the trawler, the ship shone its search lights on the *Marita Ann* and ordered it to stop. The illuminated vessel ignored the command and tried to escape by swiftly altering her course. But the fishing trawler had no hope of outrunning the *LE Emer*, or indeed the *LE Aisling*, which had promptly moved into a blockage position to prevent an escape. When warning shots were fired across the trawler's bows, the crew quickly surrendered.

Gardaí immediately climbed on board and arrested the crew of five men, among them the captain of the vessel, Martin Ferris, who was a member of the Provisional Irish Republican Army. The gardaí seized the seven-ton cargo of arms and explosives, which included 300 American-made assault rifles, 50,000 rounds of mixed ammunition, pistols, sub-machine guns, pump-action shotguns and grenades.

Having split the arrested crew among the various vessels – with Martin Ferris and Gavin Mortimer on board the *LE Emer*, John P. Crawley and John McCarthy on the *LE Aisling*, and Michael Browne on the *Marita Ann*, towed by the *LE Aisling* – the convoy, escorted by the *LE Deirdre*, set sail for Haulbowline.

Back on the Mizen, at 9.00 a.m., I was sound asleep in my bed, having come off watch at 6.00 a.m. The principal keeper, Frank Coughlan, stormed into my bedroom and told me to get up quickly if I wanted to see some history in the making. We headed out to the landing and witnessed the captured *Marita Ann* sail by, flanked by the naval fleet. Until then, we had been unaware of the military operation, as lighthouse keepers were always kept in the dark about any military procedures.

On 29 September 1985, while I was off duty for a month, the keepers on Mizen were listening to a distress and calling frequency, channel sixteen, on a VHF radio, when they picked up a May Day signal. A yacht named *Taurima* had crash-landed onto the point of Mizen Head. Its owner was Charles Haughey and he was accompanied by three other men, among them his son Conor and Vivien Nagle, a former teacher of mine. On the night, conditions were extremely calm and a dense fog hung over the area. Once the yacht crashed against the rocks, its decks broke away. Before the holed boat sank, the crew managed to send out a May Day signal, which was picked up by Richard Cummins, an SAK on Mizen Head. Then, all three men on board swiftly took to the life raft, shortly before the yacht plunged beneath the sea. The sunken vessel had originally been a fishing boat with an engine, but had later been converted to a sailing yacht.

Having summoned *The Robert* lifeboat from Baltimore, Richard Foran, the acting principal on the lighthouse, descended the north side of the cliff on a rope and landed within about 40 feet of the raft. He encouraged the four men on board to hang on in there as the lifeboat was on its way. At the time, neither he nor Richard Cummins knew that one of the men on board was Charles Haughey, who had sailed from his island of Inishvickillane. *The Robert*, under coxswain Christy Collins, transported all four men safely to Baltimore. Mr Haughey later replaced the crashed vessel with *Celtic Mist*, a 52-foot yacht that he bought for £120,000. After his death, his family gave the steel-hulled ketch as a gift to the Irish Whale and Dolphin Group.

At the time of the accident, the automation programme for lighthouses looked like becoming a reality. After the crash, in one particular television interview broadcasted on RTÉ *News*, Mr Haughey pledged that he would prevent the automation of the lighthouses. But, politics being politics, on his return to power as taoiseach in 1987 he broke his promise and the automation programme went ahead.

When I resumed duty on Mizen, about a week after the crash, I put on my diving gear, climbed down to where the yacht was lost, jumped in and dived on the sunken wreckage at the bottom of the sea. As I rummaged around in the rubble, I found an expensive, digital watch, on which I later managed to get a single reading. I gathered lots of little trinkets and pieces of cutlery, including steak knives with wooden handles. I also stumbled on a little speed log showing the distance the yacht had sailed. As I continued to search through the wreckage, I picked up a VHF radio, but quickly discarded it, as I was convinced it was damaged. However, when I spoke to other divers about it later, they told me that this particular type of radio was unlikely to be ruined by the sea, as its wiring had a protective coating, and that if it was broken it should be repairable. On my next dive on the wreck, I checked out the radio thoroughly, but it was clear that it was destroyed beyond repair, due to the constant movement of the sea.

On the sea bed, I could taste acidity in the water, as batteries from the sunken yacht had leaked. Eventually, this acidity created a hole in the tube of my breathing apparatus, causing the valve to leak air and allow the water through. In the following weeks, I picked up many more trinkets from the yacht. But as time went by, dreadful storms buried most of the remains.

Later, I gave the speed log to Richard Foran, as he had played an important part in the rescue, and I returned the digital watch to its owner Vivien Nagle. Over a period of time, I gave all the trinkets and cutlery to visitors to the lighthouse, apart from one old knife with a faded, wooden handle, which found a home in my kitchen drawer and became known as Charlie's knife.

One evening in late autumn, as I was strolling up to the lighthouse, I spotted two orca whales, known as killer whales, surging through the water at great speed. I shuddered at the thought of what would have happened if I was in the sea at that time and made up my mind there and then never again to dive in the waters around Mizen.

A year after Mr Haughey's yacht crashed, a Bridge-class ore-bulk-oil carrier, shipping thousands of tons of iron ore and crude fuel oil, found itself in dire straits near Mizen Head and posed a major threat to the environment.

13

The Kowloon Bridge

The Bridge-class ore-bulk-oil carrier was a series of six vessels built by Swan Hunter for Bibby Line, a British company engaged in shipping and marine operations. Much controversy surrounded these vessels. Only one of the fleet, the *Furness Bridge*, was constructed to the original design. Reportedly, during its sea trials, as well as its maiden and second voyages to the Persian Gulf, it suffered severe vibrations whenever it sailed at full speed. In 1971, a sister ship, the *Ocean Bridge*, narrowly escaped becoming lost and its master was killed in a serious explosion. A third Bridge-class vessel, the *Derbyshire*, disappeared off the Japanese coast in a typhoon, losing all hands on board.

Another of these tankers, the *Kowloon Bridge*, was built in 1973, measuring 965 feet in length and boasting a gross tonnage of 89,438. On 20 November 1986, during a voyage from Quebec to Scotland, the ship took shelter in Bantry Bay, after deck cracks developed in one of her frames and she lost control of her steering in heavy seas. The vessel carried a cargo of 165,000 tons of iron ore and 2,000 tons of crude, fuel oil.

Surveyors from the Department of the Marine quickly went on board to assess the situation, as the possibility of a massive oil spillage posed a major threat to the west Cork environment and wildlife.

On the Saturday, only two days after taking refuge, the ship's starboard anchor chain snapped during a sudden change of wind in the steadfast gale. The skipper of the tanker, Captain Rao, decided to ride out the storm in the open seas and the vessel drifted out towards the mouth of Bantry Bay. To make the rudder respond, the captain increased the speed of the ship and, in the teeth of a howling north-westerly gale, with winds raging at 70 miles per hour, the doomed tanker headed for Mizen Head.

That night, as the other keepers and I sat in the kitchen of the Mizen lighthouse, we heard a May Day signal from the captain, stating that the steering gear had failed and requesting immediate assistance. At that stage, the *Kowloon Bridge* was positioned about seven miles west of the lighthouse.

About 20 miles out to sea from the Mizen, a Nimrod aircraft happened to be searching for the body of a Spanish crewman who had fallen overboard from a Spanish fishing trawler. On hearing the May Day call, the Nimrod flew towards Mizen Head and circled over the *Kowloon Bridge*. It shone its search light down on the distressed vessel, lighting up one whole side of the tanker. Under the orders of the ship's captain, the crew of 28, along with two shipping company representatives, lined up on the deck and prepared to abandon the ship.

The other keepers and I went up to the point of Mizen Head to watch the ship through our binoculars. But we stayed there for only a few minutes, as the wind battered heavily against the cliff and whipped right through us, making it impossible for us to stand there any longer. We could see that the vessel was in serious trouble and heading towards disaster, as it was down by its bow.

The Nimrod continued to survey the scene and the pilot informed the ship's captain by radio that two Sea King helicopters belonging to the Royal Air Force were fuelling up at Cork airport, having searched in vain for the missing fisherman, and would fly to Mizen Head to airlift everyone on board to safety. He told the captain that he thought it was unnecessary to abandon the ship. However, he pointed out that it would have to be the captain's call.

Within only a short time, the two Sea King helicopters flew in from the east in stormy weather conditions. One hovered in mid-air, while the other began to airlift some of those on board to safety. Then, the second helicopter descended and started to airlift the remainder. By 1.00 a.m., the rescue was complete. Before the captain left the ship, he locked the steering into position, on a course heading south, at one nautical mile per hour.

Back in the kitchen of the Mizen, we monitored the situation closely by listening to the radio and we watched the fully lit ship into the early hours of the morning as it drifted south, onwards at the mercy of the turbulent seas, until it slipped over the horizon and its lights disappeared from our view.

At 3.15 p.m., the Irish naval vessel *LE Aoife* spotted the *Kowloon Bridge* south of Fastnet Rock. The naval ship stood by the abandoned vessel, which was now sailing at about five nautical miles per hour, having picked up speed, perhaps due to the swell of the ocean or the failure of its locking mechanism. At first, it seemed the vessel might drift ashore near Baltimore. Instead, it continued eastwards. At about 11.00 p.m., the tanker missed Kedge Island by 60 yards.

When the runaway ship was positioned about a half-mile from Sherkin, it turned sharp to starboard, veered right. Then it started going round continuously in huge circles. Shortly afterwards, the engines seemed to explode and a giant puff of black smoke blew out through the funnel. As the tanker was down by its bow and her engines inactive, she slowed down quickly, came to a standstill and rested motionless in the water, catching the tide.

Around 6.00 a.m. on the Monday, the *Kowloon Bridge* struck the bottom of the sea near Stag's Rock, off Toe Head. Tugs from Cork arrived swiftly on the scene, but the crews failed in their efforts to tow away the wreck, as it was too firmly wedged.

After a short while, the vessel broke its back on the reef and sank. The 2,000 tons of crude fuel oil began to leak. The colossal spillage polluted the coast all the way over to Galley Head, causing massive damage to the local environment and wildlife, particularly to beaches and sea birds. A major clean-up operation ensued.

Later, the right to the wreckage was bought for £1 by a British scrap dealer named Shaun Kent. The value of the iron ore on board was estimated at £7 million. To date, no successful salvage operation has taken place.

The *Kowloon Bridge* stands as one of Ireland's worst oil-pollution disasters and is one of the largest shipwrecks in the world by gross tonnage.

14

The Changeover

After the Falklands war, Irish Lights and English Lights introduced an automation programme, mainly because of the advances in technology and also due to an increase in air traffic and a decline in shipping. By then, fewer and bigger ships were being used to shift large quantities of cargo.

Skellig Michael lighthouse became one of the first rock stations to be automated. The lighthouse was monitored by an ultra high frequency radio signal from a mountain top in Castletownbere and the information was sent by telephone line to the central monitoring station at Irish Lights in Dún Laoghaire. Once it became obvious that the station worked well under automation, the scheme gathered pace and compulsory redundancies for lightkeepers were introduced on a last-in, first-out basis.

The automation of a lighthouse involves inserting solar lighting switches in the lighthouse to start the generators and turn on the navigation light. The optic revolving around the lighthouse is rotated constantly to prevent the sun's beams from penetrating the bull's-eye and setting it on fire. The solar photo-cell switches measure the amount of light and turn the light off and on, morning and night.

Datac is the software used to allow lighthouses become fully automated, by making them capable of being monitored and interrogated from a remote central location. If a technical fault develops at a lighthouse, an alarm notifies the computer at the central monitoring station and the computer operator sends a signal to the lighthouse to rectify the problem. If this fails, an inspector at the monitoring station issues a navigation warning for broadcast at intervals by Valentia Coast Guard Radio, until the defect is fixed by a visiting technician. All the equipment, including security equipment at a lighthouse, has multiple sensors which not only inform central control of the malfunction of a unit at the lighthouse but also identify the faulty unit. This level of interrogation ensures that the repair technicians arrive with the necessary replacement parts.

Every six hours, each station automatically phones in an update on its status. Central control can over-ride this phone-in sequence for a specific interrogation, to change over the running of one generator to another or to turn on the central heating a few days in advance of the arrival of a technician.

Other technological advances include the Automatic Identification System, known as AIS, which is an automated tracking system of shipping, capable of giving identification, movement and location. Its main purpose is to prevent shipping collisions.

With the introduction of automation, lighthouses became a back-up system, as satellites can fail and on-board equipment can break down. Lighthouses are a proven system of coastal navigation, are documented and charted, and have succeeded in keeping ships off rocks for more than 150 years.

One of the unforeseen problems and hidden costs of automation was that once the lightkeepers left the lighthouses for good, the drinking water became stagnant. As a result, when maintenance crews carried out work on any of the rock stations, Irish Lights had to fly out containers of drinking water for them.

When Mizen Head was being automated, Irish Lights offered me a transfer to the Kish lighthouse on a month-on, month-off basis for an unspecified time. But I declined. As I was then only 40 years of age and reasonably fit, I decided it was time to move on and explore new pastures. Also, I felt it would be more beneficial to my health in later years if I worked normal hours instead of irregular, shift work hours. I was happy with my decision.

Still, nostalgia set in as I began packing all my little tools into boxes, as I knew I was taking them home forever and that the days and nights of moulding ornamental weapons and model ships on lighthouses were well and truly over. For me, lightkeeping was never merely a job. It was a way of life. I felt sad to think that I might never again see many of the lightkeepers with whom I had become friends over the years, all dedicated, courageous men, who took great pride in their work.

As I closed the door of the lighthouse behind me for the very last time and crossed the arched pedestrian footbridge, I did so with a heavy heart, knowing that it signalled the end of a tradition that had lasted over 150 years and was often handed down from father to son and grandson. I thought of Frank Ryan, a principal keeper at Blackrock Mayo until 1974, whose family had the longest continuous lightkeeping association with Irish Lights, dating back to 1803.

In 1997, Ireland's automation project was complete, with the Baily becoming the last of the Irish coastal lighthouses to be automated. Fittingly, where it had all began for the lightkeepers, so too it ended.

By then, attendant lightkeepers had been appointed to check the stations every few weeks. Their duties included changing generators; filling diesel tanks; taking readings of the electronic equipment, such as battery chargers, batteries, voltage and amperage; monitoring equipment, especially the driving equipment for the lens; and checking the automatic fire-fighting gear.

Some of the attendants were boat contractors who had ferried lightkeepers, trade workers and visitors over and back from rock stations. Others were tradesmen from Irish Lights, such as Neilie O'Reilly, who succeeded Dick O'Driscoll as the attendant on Fastnet Rock. Many attendants had already worked with Irish Lights as lightkeepers, among them my father, who retired as principal keeper at Galley Head and took on the role of attendant keeper there.

Over time, the fog horn began to lose its voice, until finally, in January 2011, the last fog horn was switched off permanently, silencing the lighthouse forever. Also in 2011, the Department of Transport in Ireland announced that, after more than 200 years, the General Lighthouse Fund would cease to subsidise the maintenance of lighthouses in Ireland, thereby ending a nautical link that dated back to the 1786 Act of the Parliament of Ireland, and reflecting the fact that lighthouses are now used mainly by leisure boats, as opposed to commercial shipping vessels.

Sadly, as shipping and manual lightkeeping declined, so too my father's health began to fail. He had been a smoker all his life and had suffered mini strokes. Now, everything was catching up.

15

A Fitting Farewell

We were all there to say goodbye, except our brother Amby, who had got the news at sea and was on his way. We knew there wasn't much time left, but Daddy held on, as if he was waiting for Amby to get home.

When Amby walked in, Daddy gave him a big smile and perked up, delighted to see him. They talked for a good while, all about the countries Amby had seen. Daddy always loved when any of the lads came home from sea. Having been to sea himself, he had his own stories to tell. But he wanted to hear their stories too.

Amby was home only two hours when Daddy got a stroke. He never again spoke. I watched him die and saw a greyness start at the back of his neck and pass slowly to the front, like a cloud shading the sun. As soon as it moved right across him, his whole face changed. In an instant, he was gone.

My brother Lawrence whispered in my ear and asked me to fly the lighthouse flag at half-mast. I slipped out quietly into the dawn and raised it, without thinking why. But it said a lot, because when our neighbours rose and saw the flag at half-mast, they knew Daddy had died.

On the evening of his removal, my brothers, brothers-in-law and I shouldered his coffin from the house, out along the avenue. And as we walked slowly along, away from the sea, the lighthouse and his home, we heard the hum of the birds, among them the linnets, gold finches, martins, swallows, seagulls, kittywakes and choughs, all gathered, as if to say farewell.

On the following day, in the church of Saint Michael's in the quiet village of Rathbarry, all 15 of us sat with Mammy, who had loved Daddy always with all her heart, ever since she first laid eyes on him on Eagle Island, when he was a dashing young lightkeeper. It would be a simple funeral Mass in a simple country church for a simple jovial, wise man who had loved his family, the sea, the lighthouses and his books.

In his eulogy, Father Séamus Murphy said that he was moved to see Mammy flanked by all of her 15 sons and daughters, as it was a big tribute to Daddy and showed how much each one of us had loved and respected him. He spoke of the lifelong service Daddy had given to the sea and all who sailed on it, as well as his love for his family. As I listened, I stared at my father's closed coffin in front of the altar, with a lump in my throat, saddened that I would never see his smiling face again.

As the final hymn began and the church bell tolled solemnly, my brothers and I raised the coffin on our shoulders. We walked slowly up the aisle, followed by our grieving mother and sisters and all who had come to pay their respects. Then we laid my father to rest in the middle of the adjoining cemetery, alongside many of his old pals and neighbours. As we recited the last prayers, a gentle breeze whistled softly through the leafy green trees, reminding us that spring had come and that the cycle of life must go on, despite our loss.

And as we stood beside my father's grave, the locals came to sympathise and shake hands with us, neighbours such as Pat Joe Harrington, who was always in and out of our house, chatting to my father, and had played a part in the running of the lighthouse since he was a boy. And many came from far away too: people such as Captain Owen Deignan, an inspector at Irish Lights; and Daddy's relations from his native Wexford; as well as Mammy's relations from Ballycotton. And everyone spoke well of him, recalling when they had last met or telling some funny incident about him, easing our pain with the warmth of their memories.

As we drove back to Galley Head that evening, up the long, winding avenue, on past the neighbouring houses and in through the iron gate, we could see the flag in the distance, flying at half-mast, waving out over the jagged rocks and the swishing ocean, in the crisp March air. And as I watched the flag fly at half-mast in Daddy's honour, I imagined his spirit wafting high over the cliffs, far out to sea and way past the horizon. And I felt a terrible long-ing for him to come home, just as I had felt in Ballycotton when Edmund and I would count down the days to his homecoming and when we'd stand on the gate for hours, stretching our necks, wanting to be the first to spot him coming over the hill from the pier. And then he'd come into view, dressed in his smart, double-breasted navy-blue uniform, with two rows of gleaming brass but-tons and topped off with a matching peaked cap. And we'd race up to meet him, dance around him and breathlessly gush out every bit of our news, all in one go. Then we'd hurry him down the hill, proud as punch to have him back and eager to bring him quickly home to Mammy. But now it was different, as there would be no return. He was gone forever.

16

Fastnet Remembered

When I think back to my early days on Fastnet Rock, I always remember the principal keeper Jim, who used to stand on the balcony, motionless, gazing far out to sea, lost in his thoughts, as if he was carrying the world on his shoulders or visiting some dark corner of his mind, totally cut off from myself and the other keeper, alone in a world of his own. I never got to the root of his trouble then, as he was a quiet, introverted man, but when he died in tragic circumstances shortly afterwards, it all came to light.

During the Second World War, Jim had been a sailor in the merchant navy and was trained to take charge of a lifeboat. Once, while his ship was carrying Italian prisoners of war, it was hit by a torpedo. As the ship began to sink, the lifeboats were launched. But they were too small to take everyone on board and so some of the prisoners were left behind.

Jim packed his lifeboat to capacity. By then, the abandoned prisoners were in the water, screaming, panicking and struggling to survive. Some of them swarmed around Jim's lifeboat, striving to climb aboard, almost capsizing the vessel. Recognising the danger, Jim gave the order for the lifeboat to pull quickly away, which was the correct procedure to safeguard those on board. As the lifeboat sailed away, one of the stronger prisoners kept up with it and clung to the side with all his might. Jim pushed him away with an oar and then sadly watched him drown. The tragedy left an indelible mark on young Jim's life and the memory of the drowned prisoner haunted him for the rest of his days.

Not long after I first met Jim on Fastnet Rock, he was transferred to Eagle Island. Some months later, as he was having a pint one night in a pub in Sligo, a boat was blown up on a sand bank in stormy weather. Bravely, without any thought for their own safety, Jim and two of his friends headed to the rescue. As they rowed out towards the sand bank, a rogue wave capsized their boat. Jim held on to a mooring buoy all night long, fighting for his life, just like the Italian prisoner of war who had clung to the lifeboat. But sadly Jim drowned, along with his two courageous companions.

The sight of Jim standing on the balcony of Fastnet Rock, staring out to sea, remains fresh in my mind, as if it happened only yesterday. So too, it's hard to believe that more than three decades have passed since the Fastnet tragedy of 1979.

On the 25th anniversary of the tragic race, along with a group of people, I boarded the yacht *Inish Beg*, owned by Con Minihane, who was always a great friend of mine and was especially helpful to me when I became a fisherman after leaving Irish Lights. We sailed from Baltimore to Cape Clear, about three miles east of Fastnet, and joined the islanders and others to commemorate those who had lost their lives in the tragedy of 1979. We gathered at the foot of Leaca Mhór, a hill overlooking the harbour, as it was there that a three-foot, limestone monument had been erected to commemorate the victims of the race. Designed by Bantry stonecutter Eugene Murphy, the stone bears the names of the 15 racing sailors who perished.

Most prominent among the crowd were members of the Baltimore Lifeboat, past and present, including some of the crew who had taken part in the rescue mission, such as Kieran Cotter, who was only 24 years of age at the time of the tragedy, as well as Richard Bush and his wife Eileen, both of whom had played a vital role on the mainland during the rescue operation. I was especially delighted to meet Mrs Bushe, as I had spoken to her only once before, on that fateful night when I rang from Fastnet to ask if the lifeboat could be launched to search for the tiny vessel that had disappeared. It was fitting that she was invited to the commemoration, as until then she had never received any public recognition for her contribution to the rescue.

As the ceremony began, guest speaker Kieran Cotter recalled the part played by Baltimore Lifeboat on the night when a force 10 gale swept across the Atlantic at a terrifying speed, catching the 3,000 competitors off-guard. I was also invited to speak and recollected those horrific days and nights when a traditional, happy event turned into a nightmare and those sailing on the tumultuous seas became bombarded with waves the size of buildings. In her address, Máire Bean Uí Dhrisceoil, one of the organisers of the commemoration, said: 'The beam from the lighthouse is a constant reminder to us of the dangers of the sea. This memorial will also serve to remind future generations long after the events of 1979 have faded into distant memory.' And so, the Fastnet memorial was unveiled, listing the names of the deceased.

Other moving memorial ceremonies were held at the island's museum and also at sea. As the rain teemed down from the heavens and the sea spray sprinkled gently in the wind, boats of every description formed a flotilla on the waters off Cape Clear, just out of North Harbour, to honour those who had lost their lives in the race, including yachts, motor boats, island ferries, angling boats, the naval ship *LE Emer* as well as the *Granuaile*, with all the commissioners of Irish Lights on board, dressed in full uniform. One of the commissioners, Terence Johnson, who also held the role of second-in-command of the RNLI Ireland, made a moving speech in which he paid tribute to the victims of the Fastnet race, as well as to those involved in the rescue mission, particularly the RNLI and Irish Lights. Speeches were also made by Dr Éamon Lankford, founder and director of Cape Clear Island Museum and Archive, as well as by Father Quealy from Rockwell College, who said Mass at Cape Clear every Sunday.

The names of the 15 sailors being commemorated echoed all around, as Neil Kenefick, who had sailed in the race on Hugh Coveney's yacht, *Golden Apple of the Sun*, stood on the bow of the *LE Emer* and read their names aloud. As the bell on the *LE Emer* tolled mournfully and Kieran Cotter, coxswain of Baltimore Lifeboat, cast a memorial wreath onto the sea, his fellow crew members, along with members of Courtmacsherry Lifeboat, lined their deck in tribute to the lost seafarers.

At Cape Clear Island Museum and Archive, John P. Bourke, admiral of the Royal Ocean Racing Club, unveiled the Fastnet Race Memorial, sculptured in limestone and glass, with the names of those who died engraved on the glass, as a symbol that their names are etched forever on the sea around Fastnet Rock. The memory of those lost in the race was also honoured by the presentation of the Fastnet Race Exhibition and the launch of a book entitled *Fastnet Rock: An Charraig Aonair*, by Dr Éamon Lankford.

As I drove back home from Baltimore to Rathbarry that evening, I said a silent prayer for all who had perished at sea 25 years before. And as I reflected on the May Day calls at the time, I recollected how the distressed mariners had communicated their cries for help with great clarity, never losing their dignity as they battled for their lives on the merciless, gigantic sea. Now, they are part of a tragedy that is remembered with sadness to this very day all around the globe.

During the Fastnet race of 2011, horrific memories of the Fastnet disaster of 1979 came flooding back when a competing yacht capsized seven miles north-west of Fastnet Rock.

On Monday 15 August 2011, shortly after 5.30 p.m., the *Rambler 100*, with a crew of 21, broke its keel and overturned in seconds. Sixteen crew members hauled themselves on to the hull of the upturned 100-foot yacht, while the remaining five took to a life raft.

The stricken yacht – owned and skippered by American multi-millionaire George David – emitted a satellite distress signal, while crews of at least three other vessels sped past, unaware of their plight.

Immediately, the Irish Coast Guard launched an air and sea rescue operation, which included the Shannon and Waterford Coast Guard helicopters, the Baltimore Lifeboat, the Castletownbere Coast Guard and the naval ship *LE Ciara*, as well as ambulance crews from Kanturk and Midleton.

All 21 causalities were brought safely ashore, with those in the life raft, which had drifted dangerously towards Fastnet Rock, being the last to be located and rescued, having spent more than three hours in the water. Luckily the Valentia Coast Guard was able to pin-point their position, due to a combination of local knowledge and advanced software that predicts with wind and tide where people in the water are likely to be located.

Although the Fastnet competition of 2011 proved a stark reminder of the tragic 1979 race, the weather conditions during both events differed greatly. When the *Rambler 100* capsized, winds registered at force 5, whereas during the disaster of 1979, severe weather conditions had persisted for hours, with winds reaching storm force 10.

17

A Lesson for Life

It's strange how life can land us right back where we began, even though we might have taken many other routes in between. Today, I work at Galley Head as an attendant keeper. I took over the job from my mother, who held the post for many years after Daddy passed away. My mother lived at Galley Head for 34 years and I was there on her last day when she left for good, with her dog Minty by her side. As I locked up the iron gate and drove away from the lighthouse, I was only too aware that it was the end of an era, a time of change.

Ever since the GPS was set up in the 1980s, technological changes have continued, marking the end of the lightkeeper and altering the face of navigation. Electronic screen charts have replaced the old marine charts and the new term E navigation has been coined. Since 2004, all vessels over 300 ton must be equipped with an Automatic Identification System, known as AIS. When the AIS is superimposed on an electronic chart, it gives a 2D electronic view on the screen, showing and identifying other ships nearby. In 2009, Irish Lights set up virtual aids to navigation buoys 25 miles east of the Baily lighthouse, even though there were no buoys to be seen, they appeared on electronic charts with AIS. When I saw this on my laptop, I was amazed at how far we have progressed, and thought it fitting that it should all start again at the Baily, or is this the ghosts of supernumeraries reaching into the future?

Looking to the future, it is envisaged to have the American GPS and Russian Glonass Satellite System interoperable with the European Galileo System, which is a global navigation satellite system currently being built by the European Union and European Space Agency. All three combined will guarantee even higher accuracy positioning.

Yet, despite all the technological advancement, the lighthouses themselves remain the same, well maintained and in tip-top condition.

Often, when I go to Galley Head, I feel that time has stood still. I gaze at the picture-perfect postcard scene of the gleaming, white lighthouse and adjoining dwellings, sitting calmly on the cliff top, untouched by the swift pace of life and silent, except for the swish of the ocean and the chant of the birds. And in that peace and quiet, I hear sounds from the past, like the shrill of the whistle pipe, which was connected from the lighthouse to our parents' upstairs bedroom and was blown as a cry for help or a signal that it was time to change watch, or the whirr of the fog horn, as it gave its first kick and slowly picked up pace, until finally letting out an almighty groan. I hear my mother's laughter too, as she threw back her head and told in her native Antrim accent that she was up half the night sewing. As well as that, I hear my father, as he neatly lined up our polished shoes in the hallway, stood back with his arms folded and said with an air of contentment, 'Isn't that a grand sight now.' And I can't help but smile when I think of Pa Crowley, straightening himself up to entertain us with his mimics, 'Tea? I like a proper cup of tea.'

Inside the lighthouse, I climb up the twirling, black iron stairs, with its shiny brass rail, then step on to the balcony and look out to sea. I take in the vast oceanic landscape, with all its familiar landmarks, each of which has been eternally etched in my mind, ever since that day we moved from Mine Head and piled our belongings in the front garden, excited beyond belief at the thought of a new adventure.

Far out to sea, to the west, I see Stag's Rock, home to many shipwrecks, such as the doomed *Kowloon Bridge*, which still sits motionless on the bottom of the ocean, with its bow still intact, waiting patiently to be salvaged. Then I scan further along the coast, over to the mouth of Glandore Harbour and east to Rosscarbery Bay, where the British ship *Cecil* ran aground in dense fog in the late nineteenth century. On the same night, the *SS Crescent City*, with a cargo of bales of cotton, bags of corn and boxes of Mexican silver dollars, struck the nearby Dhulic Rock on its return maiden voyage from the states. And it was because of these two wreckages that Galley Head was built. Then, east of Dirk Bay, I see Red Strand, home to another shipwreck, the *SS Norwegian*, which hit a mine in 1917 and tragically lost six crew members. It was on Red Strand, while diving on the *SS Norwegian*, that I narrowly escaped with my life.

All my life, I'd taken risks, ever since I began flinging homemade bombs over the cliffs with Edmund, right up through all my years as a lightkeeper. In Aranmore, I had bombed the ruin of a British coastguard's house and had barely jumped out the window before it exploded like thunder. On Skellig Michael, I had climbed to its peak, without any proper mountaineering training, and nearly had my head chopped off when I walked around the back of the helicopter that had come to collect me, instead of going around the front, as I had been instructed to do. Then, on the forbidding Fastnet Rock, I had scaled up and down the lighthouse on a rope, just for fun. And, despite being light in weight, I kept battling against a whipping wind until Reggie Sugrue hauled me inside, shouting, 'Crisht you bastard get in that door!' But it was on Red Strand one summer that I took the most foolish risk of all and learned the biggest lesson of my life.

That summer, Edmund and I returned to our parents at Galley Head for our holidays. Having decided to spend our days diving, we bought some diving gear and a book entitled *Teach Yourself Underwater Swimming*. The book laid out the bare facts about swimming underwater and stated that it's possible to hold your breath underwater for three minutes.

During that particular summer, Paddy O'Sullivan, an electrician from Bandon, was salvaging copper ingots from the shipwreck of the *SS Norwegian*, which lay in about 60 feet of water a few hundred yards off Red Strand. Edmund and I joined him for our summer holidays and dived on the wreck every day.

One day, as I was preparing to dive underwater with another diver, Paddy Power, I put on one of Paddy O'Sullivan's air bottles, as my own was empty. Unlike my air bottle, which had a quick-release clasp, Paddy O'Sullivan's bottle had a leather belt with a brass buckle, like horse tackle, that fastened around the waist.

Paddy Power gave me the job of removing steel shells that were piled up on a mound, having been dug out of the wreck by an airlift. We needed to shift them about 30 feet away, as the mound was likely to tumble. The shells had been intended for use during the First World War. Each one measured about 13 inches in length and 9 inches in diameter. As they had not been primed with explosives, they were safe to handle. While Paddy Power and I dived underwater, Edmund stayed on the boat.

Walking on the ocean floor with flippers on my feet and lugging a heavy steel shell was strenuous. Shortly after we started shifting the shells, the air in my bottle expired. Instead of dropping the shell I was carrying and swimming to the surface, I suddenly remembered that the underwater swimming manual had stated that it was possible to hold your breath underwater for three minutes. So I kept walking and holding my breath. When I reached my destination, I dropped the shell. Still feeling pretty good and holding my breath, I swam over to Paddy Power and told him I was out of air and about to swim to the surface. In an instant, I began to feel hot. I knew then I was on the brink of danger. Having signalled farewell to Paddy, I started to make my way up. As I surfaced, the pressure on my body decreased. I expected that the air in my lungs would expand and give me enough oxygen to reach the surface. I was wrong. At a depth of about 10 feet, my legs stopped functioning. They felt like lead and held me back so much that I would have gladly cut them. In a matter of seconds, I became semi-conscious.

When I eventually broke the surface, I saw that I was a fair distance from the boat. Being in such a poor state, I lost my side-line vision. As a result, when I screamed for help, all I could see was the boat. Everything else was clouded in grey fog. Then I saw Edmund dive from the boat and swim in my direction. I badly needed to rid myself of the lead belt around my waist, as its weight kept pinning me down to the bottom. Luckily, it had a quick-release buckle and I was able to ditch it. But I failed to detach the empty air bottle on my back, which was preventing me from keeping my head above the surface.

As I looked up at the black cliffs of Dunowen Head, I told myself, 'Gerry, you're not going to make it this time. You're going to drown.' Now, for the first time in my life, I fully understood the superstitious fishermen who refrained from learning to swim to avoid challenging the spirits of the sea.

Instantly, I lost the will to live. The constant effort of trying to breathe in the water was draining all my energy and seemed pointless, while the temptation to end the struggle became overwhelming. But I didn't yield to it, as I could see Edmund swimming towards me and I didn't want him to find me dead.

I continued trying to breathe. I slipped down about six inches under the surface. I needed air urgently. I wriggled and twisted until I managed to lift my head above the water. I gulped some air and quickly slid back down again, too weak to stay above the surface. It seemed to go on forever, popping up and then swiftly sinking back down again.

Finally, in an uncontrolled way, I rose up to what seemed to be about waist high, expiring all of my energy and my last breath. As I slipped down for the last time, the struggle ended. I had stopped breathing. My eyes and mouth were open. I felt euphoric. It was the strangest and most enjoyable, relaxing feeling that I had ever experienced in my life.

About three feet down, Edmund reached me. He grabbed me and hauled me to the surface. By now, I had turned totally black.

Paddy O'Sullivan's rubber dinghy reached us, with Paddy and another man, Donie Calanan, on board. They dragged me into the dinghy. Both of them were shocked by the sight of me and went into a state of panic. They didn't know what to do. As the dinghy moved away, it drove over Edmund but did not hurt him. Edmund popped up from behind the boat and shouted, 'Quick! Give him the kiss of life.' On hearing Edmund's call, Paddy started to blow air into my lungs, as hard as he could. By then, Edmund had climbed on board. I don't know how many times Paddy blew into me, but my vision began to return, totally blurred, just black and white shadows. Paddy must have had a powerful pair of lungs because I thought I was going to burst from the amount of air he was blowing into me. I also felt extremely frightened, like I had been beaten up.

At this point, Paddy stopped blowing. And I gave up breathing. Then Paddy persuaded me to take a breath on my own. But it was so shallow and difficult that I decided it was a lot easier not to breathe. Paddy encouraged me again. I remember thinking, okay, just this once and that's it, no more. After much encouragement from Paddy, I began to breathe on my own, although still very weakly. Each breath got bigger. Soon, the blood started to flow again, up and down through my body. This was the most painful part of my ordeal. But it lasted for only a short while.

As the dinghy reached the landing, I kept slipping into a deep sleep, then waking up extremely alert. Edmund drove us to Doctor Hegarty in Rosscarbery. He gave me some injections, as well as a mug of hot coffee and brandy.

As I rested on the doctor's couch, I began to recover. Then I heard my father's car skid on the gravel outside, as it came to an abrupt stop. And I heard him shout, 'Where the hell is he?' I said to Edmund, 'Look, I had better be up and walking about when he gets in here, so as to make things look good.'

As he stormed down the doctor's hall, I stood inside the door of the surgery. When he looked at me puzzled, I asked, 'What is wrong with you?' Then Doctor Hegarty caught him by the shoulder and said, 'Come outside with me for a moment Larry. I need to tell you something.'

Edmund and I paced the room, wondering if the doctor could calm him. We felt as if we were two youngsters again, back in Dundalk, in trouble with the gardaí, worrying about Daddy's reaction.

Eventually, the door opened and the doctor came in, followed by Daddy. Doctor Hegarty gave us a wink. We knew then that the dust had settled and that the matter was closed, never again to be mentioned. Daddy shook hands with the doctor, then turned to us and said, 'Right so lads, we'll be off.'

When we got back to the Galley, I headed straight for the lighthouse, as I needed to be alone. I stood on the balcony, inhaled the fresh sea air and felt the soft summer breeze against my face. I fixed my eyes intently on Red Strand, now far away in the distance, unable to clutch me. It was only then that the seriousness of my escapade hit me.

Visions of my ordeal flashed before me. I saw myself in a panic, wriggling and twisting, struggling to raise my mouth above water, popping up for a second, gulping a puff of air, then slipping back down again, helpless, with the life draining out of me. I was lucky to be alive and knew it only too well.

As I replayed the incident in my mind, over and over again, I realised that humans are no match for the might of the ocean. The sea deserves our respect, at all times, as it can whip away life in the blink of an eye, without warning. On Red Strand, I had taken my eye off the ball and pushed out the boundaries too far. But I had learned my lesson the hard way and vowed never to dive again without taking proper instruction first.

I was still deep in thought, reliving my nightmare, when Edmund called me. With vivid images of Red Strand still spinning in my head, I stepped back into the lighthouse, climbed down the winding stairs and went outside. Edmund stood waiting, perched against the lighthouse, laden down with fishing gear. He handed me a timber rod and we headed off down the steep cliff, along the zig-zag path – a trail we had taken so many times before, ever since we first fished there with Daddy.

Acknowledgements

Patricia Ahern:

Writing this book would have been impossible without the help of many people and I would like to thank everyone who played a part.

Thanks especially to Gerald for sharing his life experiences with us all and for giving me the honour of co-writing the book. Always enthusiastic, committed and patient, with a sharp intellect and wit, as well as a great memory for detail, he was a pleasure to work with from beginning to end. His family background, his expertise on lightkeeping and his adventurous spirit all make him stand out from the crowd. His life has indeed been remarkable.

Thanks to Robert Sparkes, marine administration manager with Irish Lights. By introducing me to Gerald, he sowed the seeds for *The Lightkeeper*. Thanks too to John Gore-Grimes, commissioner of Irish Lights, for the beautiful foreword, and to Colm Hogan, stills photographer, for the striking front cover photograph.

Thanks also to David Givens of The Liffey Press for editing and publishing the book and for his encouragement.

Thanks to Meria Doyle for her friendship, support and hospitality, and for all the time and effort spent on organising photographs and locating research documents. Thanks also to Gerald's mother, Pauline, for giving me an insight into her fascinating life.

Many thanks too to Frank Pelly, consultant curator of the Baily Lighthouse Museum. Frank put in a huge amount of work proof-reading the book. He made excellent recommendations, gave me a memorable guided tour of the Baily lighthouse and museum and provided me with a vast amount of valuable research material, much of which was written by lightkeepers and the wives of lightkeepers, to whom I am also grateful. Thanks also to Brendan Carthy, attendant keeper at the Baily lighthouse, for being so helpful and generous with his time, and thanks to everyone at Mizen Head lighthouse, a visit to which can only be described as breathtaking.

Thanks also to Irish Lights for permission to use a map of Ireland's lighthouses and to the *Irish Examiner* and Dan Linehan, photographer, for consent to include a photograph of Gerald at Galley Head.

Also, I am especially grateful to everyone who supplied photographs and helped with the research; to authors Bill Long and Dr Éamon Lankford, whose writings provided a valuable source of reference; to Maurice Sweeney, lecturer, editor and designer, for always being on hand to give advice; to my sister Mary Lenihan for the endless hours of proof-reading and for her recommendations, and to my sister Joan Newman for her encouragement always.

Finally, thanks to my husband Denis, my sons Michael and Brian, and my daughter Fiona for all their support and for lighting up my life daily.

Thank you all.

Gerald Butler:

For years I have rejected the idea of writing this book, though I was asked to do so many times by different people, usually after a slide-show lecture on Irish Lights. I always believed that the lighthouse books were all written and, because of this belief, I never entertained the idea. Then, one day I got a phone call from Robert Sparkes, explaining to me that a lady wished to write a book and asking me if it would be okay to give her my contact details. I agreed, smiling to myself, and laughed to Robert, saying that this woman was too late, as the books were all written and the tide had run out.

Duly, Patricia rang me and called to my home. After failing to dissuade Patricia, who was so determined to do the book, I admired her enthusiasm and agreed to commit.

Then I asked Patricia if she had decided on a title for this book, and she told me in a happy voice that she had, but said I could change it if I wished. When she said the title was *The Lightkeeper*, she instantly stopped me in my tracks and, as I thought about it, I smiled at Patricia and said to her, 'That book has not been written. Well done.' What I have learned on this voyage was that if I had written this book myself it would have fallen dead. Patricia is gifted with her ability to make simple words come to life and I marvel at her talent. Thank you so much. Friends for life.

Meria, my life was like a falling star, really going nowhere, and then you popped up and turned everything around. You first showed me the secret to happiness and embraced every aspect of my life. Your interest in Irish Lights astounded me. You took pen in hand and made notes every day, making sure nothing was forgotten. Your encouragement never waned to this day. Without your help this book would have been a painful journey. I love you dearly forever.

I am grateful to my grandparents and parents for all the information and stories of your experiences that you have passed on to me about the Irish Lights, undoubtedly this charted my course. It is on your shoulders that I stand.

Thanks to my six brothers and eight sisters, growing up in your midst developed a level of confidence which carries me to this day.

Edmund, my twin, looking back on our journey, it has been great fun. All through the years, ours was a life shared. Whenever I see young twin boys, I quietly wonder if their lives are really one life. I thank God for the privilege of being your twin.

Deirdre, Teresa and Aidan, your lives are an extension of what started before my time. When I used to come home to you at the end of my term, it looked as if life was a continuing circle, only now like my father and grandfathers before me I was the Lightkeeper. Your excitement, patience and encouragement in doing this book are inspiring.

Frank Pelly came from Castlebar and when he first saw the advertisement in a paper for a job with the Irish Lights he thought they made light bulbs. Well, he filled the post in the civil side of the Irish Lights and all through his years he researched and studied Irish Lights' history. Today, he has forgotten more about CIL than everyone put together are ever likely to learn. After retiring, he is now consultant curator of the Irish Lights Museum. It is in this capacity that he really found his niche. Frank has gathered all kinds of articles from around the coast and depot and stored them in the museum. His masterpiece has to have been his ability to chronicle all the memorandum and documentation spanning two centuries. How one human being could have done all this is mind boggling. In doing my own research, you gave so generously of your time and provided me with dates and information that were invaluable in putting this book together, and then generously volunteered to help in doing corrections. A sincere and profound thanks.

David Bedlow served with Irish Lights in the Marine Department, also a storehouse of historical information, which he shared with me through many years of researching for the slide-assisted lectures that I present to historical societies, schools and elsewhere, which led to this book. Many thanks.

Robert Sparkes, now in the Marine Department, you have also helped steer me in the right directions, so much so that I sometimes felt like I had my own secretary. When dealing with the public in my capacity as attendant, you are so helpful, and a pillar of support. Many Thanks.

To all the staff in Commissioners of Irish Lights and Depot. Many Thanks.

John Gore Grimes, commissioner and diving buddy, when you joined the Irish Lights as a commissioner and arrived at the Mizen Head and asked me to go for a dive with you, I couldn't believe my ears. You amazed me with your ability to climb the sheer cliff at Mizen, lugging your heavy air bottle and gear. You reminded me of the things that I would do. You climbed to the top of Rocall and sailed your yacht around the world. When down off Cape Horn, you got off the yacht and went ashore, then climbed to the top of the cape and met some lightkeepers in a look-out post. Just the kind of commissioner that CIL needed. Many thanks for your foreword.

Maurice McCarthy, my school pal, you helped in a huge way at the beginning of my lecture trail by putting photos into slides and sharing your natural ability on doing presentations. For fifteen years, we have travelled the highways and byways of Cork together doing our lectures, you on the West Cork Railway and me on the lighthouses, culminating in this book. The journey has been great fun. Many thanks, pals for life.

Dr Éamon Lankford, Cape Clear Museum, author of *Fastnet Rock: An Charraig Aonair*, you have given me hours of advice on the phone, a tremendous help. Many thanks.

Pat Joe Harrington, you have known us longer than we know you. As young lads, we loved hanging around with you as often as we could. I often wonder how you put up with us, because what one of us didn't think of doing, the other did. You have your penance well served on this earth. I enjoy your knowledge of the Galley and locality, which has been of great help in researching for lectures and this book. Many thanks.

John Eagle, photographer and author of *An Eagle's View of Irish Lighthouses* and *Irelands' Lighthouses*, you have supplied me with a large number of your photographs that I was able to get my friend Maurice McCarthy (Clonakilty) to put into slide and use in my lectures. These were the foundation stones on which the lecture trail stood. Many thanks for all your help.

To my brother Lawrence and my sister Catherine, thanks for sending on family historical pictures. To my niece Fiona O'Donovan (*Irish Examiner*) thanks for all you help. Mary O'Brien, editor of *West Cork People*, thanks for publication and pictures. To Mary O'Driscoll, Cape Clear, thanks for photo of the Fastnet 1979 commemoration.

To Baltimore Life Boat, thanks to Cathal Cottrell and my good friend Pat Collins, both crewmen, for photographs (Fastnet 1979) and letters of commendation.

Kieran Cotter, coxwain Baltimore Lifeboat, many thanks for the help and information you have given me about the 1979 tragic yacht race. You were a crew member on the lifeboat that fateful night and your information came from experience. You were there again 32 years later when *Rambler 100* capsized, this time you were cox'n with a wealth of experience.

Dan Linehan, photographer at the *Irish Examiner*, for picture at Galley Head, many thanks.

A sincere and profound thanks to Colm Hogan, Stills Photographer, for cover pictures.

To Sharon Whooley of Harvest Films for all your help. When trying to get to Fastnet for cover photo it seemed like I was sailing against the wind. Then at the last minute you popped up out of the blue, changed my course and from then on it was plain sailing. Many Thanks.

To Neilly O'Reilly Attendant Keeper Fastnet you made it possible for the film crew to visit Fastnet for cover photo. Many Thanks.